T
tc
h in-
nocent woman is charged and brought to trial for a crime she did not commit?" He lifted a clenched fist. "It's a travesty of justice! A travesty, I tell you!" He pointed at Estelle. "This woman . . . this poor, bereaved widow who has lost the man she loved above all else in this world . . . this woman is innocent, I say! Innocent!" Parmalee pounded his fist into the palm of his other hand. "Innocent! Inn—Inn—"

Suddenly, his booming voice faltered. He took a stumbling step forward and shook his head. "Inn . . . ocent," he croaked. He turned slowly toward the jury box, and from that angle Longarm could see his face.

Parmalee's features were twisted in pain. The fist he had been pounding into his other hand was now pressed against his chest.

Judge Walton leaned forward, an anxious frown on his lined face.

"Counsel? Mr. Parmalee? Are you all right?"

Janice Parmalee was on her feet. "Father!" she screamed.

Parmalee turned one more time, muttered, "Innocent," then pitched forward on his face.

TABOR EVANS
LONGARM
AND THE
LADY LAWYER

J
JOVE BOOKS, NEW YORK

LONGARM AND THE LADY LAWYER

A Jove Book / published by arrangement with the author

PRINTING HISTORY
Jove edition / April 2002

For information address: The Berkley Publishing Group, a division of Penguin Putnam Inc., 375 Hudson Street, New York, New York 10014.

Visit our website at
www.penguinputnam.com

ISBN: 0-515-13281-0

A JOVE BOOK®
Jove Books are published by The Berkley Publishing Group, a division of Penguin Putnam Inc., 375 Hudson Street, New York, New York 10014.
JOVE and the "J" design are trademarks belonging to Penguin Putnam Inc.

PRINTED IN THE UNITED STATES OF AMERICA

10 9 8 7 6 5 4 3 2 1

Chapter 1

"Oh, my goodness," said Maureen Mullaney. "You're not going to stick that big ol' thing in little ol' me, are you, Custis?"

Longarm rolled his eyes and said, "Dadgum it, Maureen. You ain't a Southern belle any more than I am, and I damn sure ain't."

Maureen laughed. Her thick, curly red hair spread out on the pillow around her head as she lay back on the feather bed. The bed was in a room in one of Denver's finest hotels. Maureen and Longarm had come up here after sharing a late supper and a bottle of wine in a restaurant just down the street from the Opera House.

"I *am* an actress," she reminded him. "Don't you ever feel the urge to play a part every now and then?"

Longarm frowned in thought for a moment, then shook his head and said, "Nope. Reckon I'm satisfied being who I am."

"I suppose that's fine if you're a handsome, rugged U.S. marshal—"

"Deputy U.S. marshal," Longarm corrected her.

"Deputy U.S. marshal," said Maureen. "It doesn't really matter, does it?"

Longarm said, "It might to my boss, Billy Vail. He's the chief marshal for this district."

Maureen cupped her naked breasts, lifting them and squeezing them so that the large red nipples were prominent. "Why are we talking about this right now, Custis? Can't you see that I'm aching to have you make love to me?"

Longarm's manhood, which was jutting out hard and proud from his groin, gave a little jump at that question. He lowered himself to the bed, moving into position over Maureen, who spread her thighs even more in invitation. Longarm looked in appreciation at the triangular thicket of dark red hair that pointed irresistibly toward the pink folds of her femininity. In the light from the lamp on the small table next to the bed, he saw tiny drops of moisture glittering like diamonds among the fine-spun hair.

Maureen took hold of Longarm's shaft and brought the head of it to the gates of her womanhood. She rubbed the tip of it up and down the juicy cleft. Longarm's jaw tightened with the need to plunge himself into her. He resisted, though. He hadn't seen Maureen for months, so he wanted their rendezvous to be as long and delicious as possible.

He had first met Maureen in Kansas City, Missouri, while she was performing with Colonel Jasper Pettigrew's Wild West Show and Frontier Extravaganza. One of Longarm's cases had gotten him mixed up with Colonel Pettigrew's troupe of showmen, and he and Maureen had shared times of both danger and passion. The Wild West Show had broken up at the end of that assignment, and Maureen had moved on to other things. At present she was part of a traveling Shakespearean troupe that had come to Denver to put on some of the Bard's plays at the Opera House. Longarm had seen her name and picture on one of the troupe's advertising posters and recognized her immediately.

He had been in the front row that night to watch her play Ophelia in *Hamlet,* a part that he considered not to do her justice because it didn't showcase her feisty nature. But she performed it well, as he expected. Afterward, he'd gone backstage to say hello, and she'd practically jumped into his arms with a squeal and a kiss. "I was hoping I'd see you while we were in town," she had told him.

From there, it had been natural for them to go out for supper, and after that to come back here to Maureen's hotel room. Their previous times together had taught them that they were a good match for each other. If anything, Longarm reflected, Maureen was even lustier than he was. Must have been that red hair and her Irish temperament.

Now he decided that she had teased him long enough. With a thrust of his hips, he sheathed his throbbing organ inside her. Maureen gasped in pleasure as he filled her. Longarm's hips pumped, making his shaft slide wetly in and out of her. The juices seeping from her core drenched his long, thick pole of male flesh.

"Ride me, Custis!" she ground out as she turned her head from side to side, dizzy from the pleasure he was giving her. "Ride me!"

Longarm brought his head down to hers and found her mouth with his. Her breasts flattened against his broad chest as he kissed her. Brazenly, she parted her lips and drove her tongue into his mouth. To Longarm, she tasted as hot as fire and as sweet as strawberries.

After several minutes, Longarm pushed himself up and balanced on his knees while he lifted Maureen's legs and rested her muscular calves on his shoulders. He managed to stay inside her while he was doing that, and once she was in the new position, he was able to drive even farther into her. Her sheath stretched to accommodate this deeper penetration. She cried out as he plumbed depths within her that only he had ever been able to reach.

"Oh, yes, Custis!" she said in a half-moan. "Give me all of it!"

Longarm obliged, plunging into her as deep as was humanly possible. Maureen began to spasm as her climax rolled over her. Her inner muscles clutched at Longarm's shaft with incredible strength, like a giant hand trying to milk his seed out of him. With an effort of will, he fought off the urge to empty himself inside her.

Maureen shuddered again and again, each tremor a little weaker than the one before it. Finally, she gave one last shiver. Her eyes were closed in contentment. Longarm held himself where he was, satisfied for the moment to look down at Maureen's lovely face with its spray of tiny, almost unnoticeable freckles. Her breasts with their crinkled nipples rose and fell rapidly as she tried to catch her breath.

At last, she opened her eyes and looked up at him with a deep, abiding happiness in those green orbs. "Custis . . . ," she whispered. Then, as a new realization hit her, she said, "Custis, did you . . . you didn't . . . ?"

"Nope," he said with a grin, and his organ throbbed and swelled anew as he began sliding it in and out of her.

"Oh, my God!" she wailed as a fresh wave of sensation burst inside her, even stronger than the one before. It peaked and fell, peaked and fell, in a seemingly endless series of passionate explosions, and Longarm could tell when each of them erupted. When neither of them could stand any more, he buried himself fully within her again and allowed his own climax to come to the boiling point. His seed began to spurt into her in thick, superheated jets. Each one set her off again.

Longarm finished, and every muscle in his body seemed to go limp except for the one that was still embedded inside Maureen's female core. Carefully, he lowered her legs off his shoulders and withdrew his shaft. Maureen was gasping for air as if she had just run a mile or more. Longarm stretched out beside her, and after a moment she rolled onto her side and snuggled against him. He reached down and drew the sheet over both of them, enjoying the feel of its clean crispness against his momentarily supersensitive skin.

"Oh, Custis, I've missed you so much," she said as she rested her head on his shoulder. "There's never been anyone else like you."

He kissed her on the forehead. "I'm mighty fond of you, too."

She laughed softly. "But neither of us is going to pretend that there's never anyone else in our lives, are we?"

"Wouldn't be much point in that."

"No, I don't suppose there would. I'm just grateful for the time we have together."

"Me, too," said Longarm, and that was as honest as honest could get. He was right fond of Maureen.

After a few minutes of companionable silence, she said, "The troupe leaves next week for San Francisco."

"I know."

"So we should make the most of the time we have, shouldn't we?"

Longarm reached over and cupped one of her breasts, filling his hand with the firm, creamy globe. His thumb found the hard nipple and caressed it.

"That's just what I was thinking," he said.

As Longarm walked along Denver's darkened streets later that night, he wondered, not for the first time in his life, if a fella and a gal could actually screw themselves to death if they tried hard enough.

It was a good thing Maureen was only going to be in Denver for a few more days, he reflected, or he might get the chance to find out.

He was tired, exhausted actually, but it was a good sort of weariness. He could have spent the night in Maureen's hotel room. She wouldn't have minded, scandalous though it might be for her to have an overnight male guest. As an actress, she was accustomed to scandal. But Billy Vail was expecting him at nine o'clock in the morning, and Longarm figured he would be more likely to arrive at the chief marshal's office on time if he spent the rest of the night in his rented room on the other side of Cherry Creek.

Of course, he'd been late before and it hadn't killed either him or Billy, but contrary to his boss's opinion, Longarm didn't sit around thinking up ways to deliberately infuriate Vail. Most of the time, it just sort of happened that way.

He reached into his vest pocket, slid out a cheroot, and lit it with a lucifer that he snapped into life with an iron-hard thumbnail. He shook out the sulfur match and dropped it to the cobblestones, then inhaled deeply, dragging the smoke into his lungs. A moment later, he blew it out in a near-perfect smoke ring that was quickly shredded and carried away by the gentle night breeze.

Longarm hoped that Billy Vail didn't want to hand him a new assignment that would take him out of Denver before Maureen had to leave. Since they got to spend so little time together, it would be a shame if his job caused them to miss any of it. But he supposed things like that went with packing a badge for Uncle Sam. He had known the job could be damned inconvenient when he took it, not to mention dangerous.

He was strolling along a tree-lined street in one of the city's best neighborhoods. The fragrance of night-blooming flowers was in the air. This was sort of the long way around to get back to his place, but it was a warm night and, despite his tiredness, he felt like walking. His body might be weary, but the time he'd spent with Maureen had invigorated his mind. He kept thinking about her and wondering if he had made a mistake by not staying the night in her hotel room.

He was so preoccupied with those thoughts that he almost didn't hear the scream that cut through the night like a knife blade. Almost. But his lawman's instincts wouldn't allow him to ignore it.

His head came up sharply as he heard the terrified shriek. His teeth clenched tight on the cheroot, and his hand moved to the butt of his Colt .45 Peacemaker, holstered on his left hip in a cross-draw rig. He pivoted toward the source of the unholy sound, which seemed to be the large mansion he was passing on the left side of the street.

The front door of the house banged open violently, and a figure darted out. Flowing white garments stood out sharply against the shadows that clogged the front yard of the estate. Longarm didn't know off the top of his head who owned this place, but most of the gents who had houses along here were mine owners, bankers and financiers, railroad magnates, or the like.

The woman who had burst out of the house screamed again as she raced along the flagstone walk toward the street. Longarm spit out the cheroot and moved to intercept her. He didn't know if she was crazy or scared or what was the matter with her, but she was liable to hurt herself if she went plunging out into the street like that. His long legs carried him forward quickly, and he reached the open front gate of the estate at the same time she did.

Longarm reached out to grab her as she almost ran headlong into him. The woman was moving so fast he stumbled a little as he brought her to a sudden stop. "Hold it!" Longarm said urgently. "Just hold on there, ma'am. What's wrong?"

In the poor light, Longarm couldn't tell much about her, but he had the sense that she was attractive. Light-colored hair hung loosely around her shoulders, and the white robes she wore were nightclothes. The garments weren't totally white, Longarm saw now. They had ominously dark blotches scattered on them.

Panic-stricken at being grabbed like that, she cried out and tried to jerk away from him, but she was no match for his strength. Longarm took hold of her upper arms and gave her a shake. Whatever was wrong, he couldn't help her if she was too hysterical to tell him about it.

"Settle down, ma'am," he said in a low, urgent voice. "I'm a lawman. I'll help you if you'll just tell me what's wrong."

His calming words seemed to get through to her brain. She turned her face to him and said, "Y-you're a l-lawman?"

"That's right. What's happened here?"

A great shudder went through the woman, and she half-turned in Longarm's grip to point back toward the mansion. "He's in there," she said shakily. "He . . . he's dead! Murdered!"

Chapter 2

Murder was a mighty serious accusation, thought Longarm as he held the terrified woman, but an even more serious crime if it actually had been committed. "Where?" he demanded. "Who's been hurt?" The victim might not be dead, only injured.

The woman pointed with a shaking finger toward the house. "I-in there! Down the hall on the left . . . in the library . . . He's my husband . . . Oh, dear Lord!"

That set her off on another bout of wailing. Longarm gritted his teeth, shook her again, and asked, "Is anybody else in there?"

"I . . . I don't know . . . Oh, no, oh, no, I can't bear it—!"

Longarm restrained the impatience he felt. If this lady was right and her husband had been killed, he couldn't blame her for being upset, especially as it appeared probable she had discovered the body. He put her aside and ordered, "Wait here. I'll go in and see about this."

He didn't know if she would do as he told her or not, but since he was alone there was nothing else he could do except stride toward the mansion and hope for the best. He wanted to get inside and locate the woman's husband, just in case he was still alive.

Longarm drew his gun as he walked in the front door

of the house, which was still open after the woman fled through it. He paused in the ornately decorated foyer to listen and have a look around. The house was quiet, at least for the moment.

To his left opened an opulently furnished parlor that was almost large enough to be a ballroom. It was dark at the moment, but the light from the wall lamp in the foyer spilled into it and reflected off crystal chandeliers hung from the ceiling. To the right was a closed door of thick mahogany, and ahead of Longarm stretched a long hallway that led toward the rear of the house. The corridor was lit by small, gold-plated lamps set in brass wall sconces. The walls were hung with pictures, some of them portraits and the others landscapes. Everything looked expensive, from the beamed ceilings, to the wallpaper with its delicate, flowery tracings, to the thick rug that muffled Longarm's steps as he started down the hallway toward a door on the left that stood open. A slanting rectangle of light came from beyond the open door and lay across the corridor.

Longarm's natural caution, developed over years in a dangerous business, prompted him to have the Colt leveled and ready for instant use as he stepped quickly through the door and dropped into a crouch. He swiveled from side to side, his keen eyes checking the room for a possible threat. He didn't see any.

The room was a library, as the woman had said. The walls were lined with floor-to-ceiling bookshelves, except for an area that a large fireplace took up on one wall. There was no fire in the hearth now, since it was summer.

An impressive desk sat in the middle of the room, its polished hardwood top littered with a scattering of papers. The flame in a lamp sitting on the desk was turned up high. To the left of the desk was a free-standing bar, while to the right was a massive table with a marble-inlaid top. A thick, leather-bound volume that Longarm recognized as a dictionary sat on the table, along with a large globe.

Both items had the look of being there more for show than for actual use.

The corpse lying on the rug in front of the desk certainly wasn't very decorative, however. The body belonged to a man in late middle age. In life he would have been imposingly handsome, with tanned, rugged features and a leonine shock of silvery hair. Death had stolen any attractiveness from his features, leaving them twisted and frozen in pain and disbelief. He wore a belted, silken dressing gown over a nightshirt. Bare, hairy calves and feet shod in soft slippers protruded from the bottom of the garments.

The dead man lay on his back, staring sightlessly at the ceiling. The handle of a knife stuck up from his chest. Hardly aware that he was paying attention to such details, Longarm automatically noted that the knife handle was made from carved bone. The blade had been plunged deeply into the man's chest, almost to the hilt. A large, fresh bloodstain surrounded the wound.

Longarm had known as soon as he saw the corpse that the man was dead. There was no mistaking the lifeless pallor of the man's face. Longarm knew as well that the woman had been right about this being a case of murder. It was just barely possible that a fella could have stuck a knife that deep in his own chest, but it was mighty unlikely as far as Longarm was concerned.

No one else was in the library. Longarm holstered his gun and moved closer to the body. He went to one knee beside it and studied the dead man's face. Something about this hombre was familiar, thought Longarm. He had seen the man somewhere before, or at least a picture of him . . .

A name popped out of Longarm's memory: Jericho Malone. Once he had recalled that, the rest of it came back to him. As befitted the street on which he lived, Jericho Malone was a rich, rich man. He had made his fortune by discovering a silver lode in the mountains southwest of Denver. Longarm didn't remember the name of Malone's mine, but he knew it was lucrative. As one of the silver barons who called Denver home, Malone's picture was often in the newspapers, usually attending this or that ball, or some performance of the opera, or some other social event, always in the company of his wife . . .

"Ohhhh!" The pitiful wail came from the doorway of the library. "It's true, it's really true. He's dead!"

Longarm looked in that direction and saw that the woman had followed him into the house. That didn't really surprise him. He hadn't thought she would stay out. He came to his feet and started toward her. She moved farther into the library, her steps jerky and halting. Now, in the light, he could see that the dark blotches on her gown and robe were bloodstains, just as he had thought.

"Mrs. Malone?" he said. The woman had her hands pressed to her mouth, and her eyes were wide and staring. When she didn't reply to his words, Longarm said more urgently, "Mrs. Malone?"

She finally blinked, and her eyes moved over to him. "Yes, I . . . I'm Mrs. Malone," she said raggedly.

"That's your husband, isn't it? Jericho Malone?"

"Yes, I—"

A rapid patter of footsteps in the hall interrupted her. A man appeared suddenly in the doorway. He was short, pudgy, and round-faced, with thinning dark hair pomaded to his skull. He was about as unthreatening an individual as Longarm had seen in a while . . . or, at least, he would have been if he hadn't been waving around a small revolver.

He burst out, "Who—what—" and jerked the revolver toward Longarm. Longarm bit back a curse and flung himself forward as he saw the little man's finger begin to tighten on the trigger.

Longarm slapped the weapon aside just as it cracked spitefully. The gun went spinning out of the little man's hand. Longarm grabbed the lapels of the man's coat and shoved him backward, actually lifting him off his feet by the coat as he forced him back against the wall. The little man let out a frightened squeak.

"I don't take kindly to folks pointing guns at me, old son," Longarm grated as he held the man against the wall. "I like it even less when they actually shoot at me."

"Uh . . . unhand me, you hooligan!" the man struggled to get out of Longarm's grip. "I'll have the law on you!"

"I *am* the law," said Longarm. "Who the hell are you?"

The woman said, "Howard . . ." and took a step toward them, one hand outstretched.

"Keep her away from me!" the man practically screeched. "Don't let her kill me, too!" He stared wild-eyed at Longarm. "For God's sake, if you're really a lawman, *do something!*"

Longarm was ready to do something, all right. He turned away from the wall, taking the little man with him. He shoved the man into an overstuffed armchair near the fireplace and pointed a finger at him. "Stay there!" he barked. He turned back to the woman. "Mrs. Malone, what happened here?"

Before she could answer, the man in the armchair said excitedly, "What happened? I'll tell you what happened! She killed him, that's what happened!"

Longarm turned his head and shouted at the man. "Hush up!" To the woman, he said in much quieter tones, "What about it, Mrs. Malone? I know this is a mighty bad time, but I need to know what went on here tonight."

Actually, what he needed to do, Longarm told himself, was to send for the Denver police and let them take over. Murder was a state crime, not a federal one, and unless what had happened here tonight had some connection to the federal government, which seemed unlikely, Longarm was out of his bailiwick. But he was also curious, not to mention a duly authorized representative of the law, so it wouldn't hurt to carry on a little preliminary questioning.

Mrs. Malone wouldn't look at her husband's body. Her haunted eyes rested anywhere and everywhere in the room except on the corpse lying in front of the desk. She said,

"I . . . I don't know what happened. I just came in and found Jericho there . . ."

"That's a lie!" burst out the small man. "I came into the room and saw her kneeling over Mr. Malone with the knife in her hand! She killed him, I tell you! And I was afraid she'd come after me next, so I went to fetch my gun."

Longarm glared at him. "If that's true, why'd you try to take a shot at me?"

"I . . . I didn't really mean to." The man looked somewhat embarrassed now. "You were just so . . . so big and threatening-looking. When I came into the room and saw you standing there, I . . . I suppose I panicked." He reached into his vest pocket and pulled out a handkerchief. After mopping sweat off his forehead, he went on, "I'm not accustomed to this sort of thing."

"That ain't a good enough reason for throwin' down on a fella," Longarm said sternly. "You're damned lucky I didn't haul out my own hogleg and ventilate you."

The little man swallowed and turned pale, as if he had just realized what a bad mistake he had made by pulling a gun on this tall, rangy, dangerous-looking stranger.

Again, Longarm turned back to the woman. Now that he'd had a chance to get a better look at her, he saw that his first impression was right—she was quite attractive. She was around thirty years old and had thick, ash-blond hair framing pale, elegant features. The nightclothes she wore clung to her slender figure. Longarm could see the woman's nipples standing out against the thin fabric.

"Maybe we ought to go somewhere else to talk," he suggested. Mrs. Malone might feel better if she could get out of the room where her husband's body lay cooling. He didn't much like the idea of leaving the corpse unattended, though.

She shook her head. "No, I . . . I'm better now," she said. "This is all so terrible I can barely grasp it, but I . . . I have to be strong." She took a deep breath. "Could I ask who you are?"

"Deputy United States Marshal Custis Long," Longarm told her. "I can show you my badge and bona fides, if you want."

"No, that's all right, Marshal, I believe you. But shouldn't the local authorities be summoned?"

Now she was starting to think along the same lines as he was. He nodded and said, "Are there any servants in the house?"

"The cook and the gardener . . . they're married . . . they live out back in a small cottage . . ."

"In a few minutes, we'll get them up and send the gardener for the Denver police. Right now, though, I want you to tell me what happened."

"A short time ago, I came into this room looking for my husband. I . . . I knew Jericho was doing some work . . ." She gestured vaguely toward the papers on the desk. "I found him like that, lying on the rug with the knife . . . oh, God . . . with the knife . . ."

Longarm thought that Mrs. Malone's hard-won control was about to slip away from her again. Before it could, the small man in the armchair, who had been fidgeting impatiently, said, "That's not the way it was. I saw her with the knife, I tell you. She stabbed him, Marshal."

Tears rolled down the woman's face as she turned to look at the man. "How can you accuse me of such a thing, Howard? How? What did I ever do to deserve such . . . such betrayal?"

"I'm not betraying you," the little man said coldly. "Mr. Malone was my employer, but even more than that, he was my friend. And *you* killed him."

Keeping a tight rein on his temper, Longarm asked, "Just who in blazes are you, old son?"

The little man drew himself up so that he was sitting straighter in the armchair. "My name is Howard Summerlin," he told Longarm. "I was Mr. Malone's private secretary."

"Well, Howard, keep your trap shut until I get finished with the lady, all right?" Longarm's tone was affable as he made the suggestion, but it had an icy edge underneath the words. Howard Summerlin frowned at the rebuke but drew back in the chair as if he intended to be quiet for a while.

"You *are* Mrs. Malone?" Longarm said to the woman.

She wiped away some of the tears with her hand. "Yes, I'm Estelle Malone. I was Jericho's wife."

"*Second* wife," muttered Howard Summerlin. Longarm shot him a narrow-eyed glance, and he didn't say anything else.

"What's all this about you having the knife in your hand?"

"It's true," Estelle Malone said.

That admission came as something of a surprise to Longarm. "Are you saying that you did stab your husband, ma'am?"

"No, of course not." She hugged herself and shuddered at the memories that had to be going through her head. "When I . . . when I came into the room and saw Jericho lying there, I saw the knife and knew he was hurt. I ran to his side and threw myself down. I tried to see if he was still breathing. To see if he was still . . . alive." Mrs. Malone looked down at the bloodstains on her garments. "I suppose that's when I got this blood on my clothes. I . . . I was lying atop Jericho, you see . . ."

She started to tremble, and Longarm said, "Take your time."

After a moment, Estelle was able to go on. "I took hold of the knife," she said. "That much of what Howard has told you is true, Marshal. My instincts were telling me to . . . to pull it out of Jericho's chest. But then I thought that if he *was* still alive, I might just hurt him worse by removing the knife. That was when Howard came in and saw me."

Longarm swung toward Summerlin. "Is that how it was?"

Summerlin hesitated and fidgeted some more. Finally, he said, "She was kneeling beside him, practically lying on top of him. And she had the knife in her hand, just like I told you."

"But was it already stuck in his chest?"

"I . . . I don't recall. I was so shocked. I'm afraid I reacted badly. I'm not accustomed to violence, as I told you."

"He shouted at me, called me a murderer, and then ran out," Estelle said. "When I heard that word . . . *murderer* . . . I think that was when I finally realized that Jericho was dead. I'm not sure what happened then. I remember screaming, and I ran out of the room. I . . . I just had to get away . . . I ran . . ."

"You ran out into the street and right into me," said Longarm.

"Yes. I ran right into a lawman. I suppose that was lucky, wasn't it?"

Longarm glanced at the corpse and thought that there hadn't been much luck in or around this house tonight except the bad kind.

He put a hand on Estelle Malone's arm and started steering her toward the door of the library. "You'd better go get the gardener now and have him fetch the Denver police."

"What about me?" Howard Summerlin asked from the chair by the fireplace.

Without looking back at him, Longarm said, "You and me'll stay right here to watch over things."

To watch over the body of Jericho Malone, that was what he meant, thought Longarm, and all of them knew it.

"You'd better not let Mrs. Malone out of your sight," Summerlin said. "She'll run off and you'll never see her again. She'll flee like the killer she is."

Longarm was about to snap at Summerlin when he heard new footsteps in the hall. Maybe the servants had finally noticed the commotion in the house and come to see what was going on. If that was the case, it would sure simplify matters.

But it wasn't the gardener or the cook who suddenly appeared in the doorway to stare aghast into the room. It was a lovely young woman in evening clothes, a red gown and a red hat perched on an upswept mass of brunette curls.

And when her shocked gaze fell on Jericho Malone's body, she shrieked, *"Daddy!"*

Chapter 3

Barely skipping a beat, the beautiful newcomer switched her gaze to Estelle Malone and screeched, "You bitch! You finally killed him!" She flung herself at Estelle, the fingers of her gloved hands hooked like claws as they reached for the older woman's face.

Longarm didn't wait to see if Estelle was going to defend herself. He pushed her behind him and moved to intercept the furious young woman. He caught hold of her wrists and said firmly, "Hold on there, miss."

She twisted in his grip and tried to pull away from him. "Let go of me!" she practically spat. "Let me at her! I'll kill her—"

"Stop it!" Longarm said. "There's been enough killin' here tonight."

"I didn't do this, Natalie," Estelle Malone said. "I found your father like this, I swear I did."

"Liar!" Curses spewed from Natalie Malone's mouth, all of them directed at her stepmother. Longarm reckoned Natalie hadn't learned those words at the sort of fancy finishing school to which her father had probably sent her.

He was figuring things out on the fly. Obviously, Natalie was Jericho Malone's daughter, and equally obviously from their ages and from what Howard Summerlin had said about Estelle being Malone's second wife, Estelle was not Natalie's mother. And the most obvious thing of all, reflected Longarm, was that Natalie hated Estelle with a passion.

He stepped into the hall, pulling Natalie with him. "Come on, miss," he said. "You don't need to be in there."

"Who the hell are you?" Natalie demanded. Her brown eyes flashed with anger. "And let go of me!"

"Not until you promise you ain't goin' to run back in there and raise a ruckus. As for who I am, my name's Custis Long. I'm a deputy U.S. marshal."

Natalie Malone was filled with grief and anger, but Longarm's words finally got through to her fevered brain. She looked at him and said, "You're a U.S. marshal?"

He didn't bother correcting her. He just nodded and said, "The situation's under control, Miss Malone. I was just about to send for the Denver police. Why don't you go back down the hall to the parlor and wait for me there?"

"My father . . ." Tears welled from her eyes and rolled down her cheeks. "Is he . . . is he . . ."

Longarm nodded solemnly. "I'm afraid so."

Natalie glanced past Longarm toward the library door, and her voice was ice cold as she said quietly, "She did it, you know. She killed him."

"We'll see about it," Longarm promised. "Right now I want you to just go have a seat and try to calm down."

Natalie drew a deep, shaky breath. "All right."

Longarm let go of her wrists, and she darted past him in the blink of an eye. He made a grab for her but missed. "Damn it!" he said as he started after her.

Natalie raced through the open door into the library. Longarm heard a scream as he pounded into the room. Natalie had tackled Estelle, and both women were rolling around on the floor while Howard Summerlin, who had gotten up out of the chair by the fireplace, stood by, moving around nervously and looking unsure what to do next.

Longarm bent over the struggling women and saw a flash of thigh as Estelle's nightclothes rode up her legs. Under other circumstances he probably would have appreciated the view, but not now. Since Natalie was the aggressor, he hooked his hands under her arms and hauled her up and off of Estelle.

"Damn it!" he said again. "You promised me you wouldn't do that, Miss Malone."

Natalie's hat had come off and her brown hair was loose now, falling around her face and shoulders. She flailed at Estelle as Longarm held her back. "The witch! The dirty, filthy, murdering witch!"

Estelle climbed shakily to her feet. She shook her head and began, "I swear, Natalie—"

Once more Natalie interrupted with a stream of profanity. Howard Summerlin looked profoundly shocked, not to mention a little frightened, by what he was seeing and hearing. Longarm was just frustrated. He pulled Natalie toward the door of the library. "Summerlin, you go fetch the gardener and send him for the police," Longarm said. "Can you do that?"

The little man swallowed and nodded. "Of course."

"Mrs. Malone," Longarm said to Estelle, "do I have your word that you'll go up to your room and stay there?"

Estelle nodded. "Certainly."

"Don't believe her!" Natalie cried. "She's lying!"

"You come along with me, miss." Longarm didn't intend to let Natalie out of his sight again until after the police arrived and had things under control.

He steered the young woman into the corridor, uncomfortably aware that the way his arms were wrapped around her from behind, they were mighty close to the thrust of her breasts. Her rear end bumped against his groin a time or two, as well, as he wrestled her out of the library. He stopped about ten feet away from the open door, where he could still keep an eye on it by glancing over his shoulder. Howard Summerlin left the room hurriedly. Estelle Malone followed at a slower pace, hugging herself and shivering slightly even though the evening was quite warm. She went toward the back of the house, evidently bound for a rear staircase that would lead up to her bedroom.

Longarm didn't let go of Natalie Malone until the two of them were alone in the hall. Then he released her and stepped back. She spun around to confront him, her eyes blazing with fury.

"How dare you interfere?" she demanded. "This is between me and that . . . that harpy!"

"That's where you're wrong," he told her. "It's a matter for the law now."

"Because my . . . my father was murdered—" Natalie suddenly covered her face with her hands and began to sob. Her shoulders shook with the depth of the emotions she felt.

Longarm watched her warily, not totally convinced at first that this wasn't another act. After a few moments, though, he realized that Natalie really was in the grasp of utter grief and despair. Either that, or she was a better actress than anybody Longarm had ever seen, up to and including Sarah Bernhardt and Maureen Mullaney.

His chivalrous instincts urged him to step forward and put his arms around her in an attempt to comfort her, but he restrained the impulse. For one thing, he didn't even know the gal, and for another, she was sort of mad at him right now. He thought about lighting up a cheroot to replace the one he had dropped outside, but he figured the time wasn't right for that, either.

A few minutes went by, and Natalie's sobs trailed off to a series of sniffles. She looked at Longarm, her eyes red now from crying, and said calmly, "She really did do it, you know."

Thinking that she might be rational enough now to answer a few questions, Longarm asked, "Why do you say that?"

"Because they hated each other. Father wanted a divorce, but Estelle refused to give him one."

"She *is* your stepmother, ain't she?"

Natalie nodded. "That's right. My mother passed away fifteen years ago, when I was five."

"How long ago did your father marry the current Mrs. Malone?"

"Three years ago."

Longarm did some ciphering in his head, then asked, "You have any brothers or sisters?"

Natalie shook her head, clearly wondering why he had asked that question. "No, I'm an only child."

So she'd had her papa to herself for a dozen years since the death of her mother, thought Longarm. Jericho Malone was a rich man, so he'd probably spoiled Natalie. It would be a natural thing for a widower with only one child to do.

Then another woman had shown up, moved into the house, and probably, in Natalie's eyes, taken her father away from her. No wonder the two of them hadn't gotten along very well.

But whether Natalie was prejudiced against her stepmother or not, there might still be some truth to what she said.

"You said your father wanted a divorce," Longarm went on. "Why?"

"Because Estelle is insanely jealous. She accused Father of . . . of having a mistress." Natalie sniffled again, then lifted her chin defiantly. "That's impossible. My father is . . . was . . . an honorable man." The tears started to flow more freely again as her words reminded her that her father was dead.

Longarm figured the idea of a silver baron like Malone having a ladyfriend on the side wasn't as farfetched as Natalie seemed to think it was, but he had to admit that he hadn't known the man. Maybe Malone really had been the pillar of virtue his daughter supposed him to be.

"That didn't stop Estelle from making his life a living hell," Natalie went on after wiping her eyes. "She badgered him constantly, always making accusations, even having him followed. It was terrible."

"If that's the way she felt, how come she didn't want to give him a divorce?"

Natalie shook her head again. "She said that would be too easy on him. She said she wasn't going to give him what he wanted. They fought about it all the time." She looked intently at Longarm. "Can you blame me for hating her?"

"I sort of walked blind into this, Miss Malone," Longarm told her. "I ain't blaming anybody for anything just yet."

He kept casting glances over his shoulder at the door to the library. Nobody had been in or out of the room since they'd all vacated it a short time earlier. Jericho Malone was lying in there—alone in death, as everybody wound up sooner or later. Longarm wondered what the last sight was the murdered man had seen. Had it been the face of his killer? It seemed as if Longarm's profession brought him face-to-face with death at least once a month, so that he and the Grim Reaper were old saddle pards by now. And yet Longarm knew nothing of what lay beyond the veil, no more than did anyone else who still drew breath.

He frowned. Such things wouldn't do with too much pondering. That was a good way for a fella to give himself a headache.

Footsteps made him glance back again, and for a split-second, he had the crazy idea that Jericho Malone had somehow come to life and was walking out of the library. The doorway to the room was still empty, however. Coming along the hall from the rear of the house was Howard Summerlin. He had his handkerchief out and was mopping his forehead again.

"I've sent Carlson for the authorities," Summerlin said. "He's the gardener. His wife insisted on going up to see about Mrs. Malone. I hope that's all right."

Longarm nodded. "I reckon so."

Natalie spoke up. "Howard, you know that Estelle must have done this . . . this dreadful thing, don't you?"

"I saw her with the knife in her hand," Summerlin replied. He nodded toward Longarm. "The marshal knows all about it."

"Is that true, Marshal?"

Longarm shrugged. "Mrs. Malone claims she touched the knife when she found her husband already stabbed."

"She's lying! Why haven't you already arrested her?"

"For one thing, it ain't been established who's lying and who ain't," Longarm said. "For another, in a case like this, it's up to the Denver police to make any arrests—"

The front door swung open, interrupting him, and several men came into the foyer. One of them was wearing trousers and a coat hastily pulled on over a nightshirt, so Longarm figured he was the gardener who had been sent to bring the police.

The man who seemed to be in charge of the group was short and stocky, with a beefy, clean-shaven face. He wore a brown tweed suit and a dark brown derby. When he took off the hat, he revealed graying dark hair. He came down the hallway toward Longarm, Natalie, and Summerlin. His hat was in his left hand. He extended the right to Longarm.

"Hello, Marshal," he said. "I didn't expect to find you here. Does Billy Vail's office have an interest in this case?"

Longarm shook hands with the man as he replied, "Nope. Billy don't know a thing about it. I reckon you can say I'm just a witness this time around. I sort of stumbled in on it accidental-like."

"I see."

Longarm turned to Natalie and Summerlin. "This here is Daniel Hubbard. He's a detective on the Denver police force. Dan, this is Miss Natalie Malone and Mr. Howard Summerlin."

Hubbard inclined his head toward Natalie. "My sympathy on your loss, Miss Malone," he said. Clearly, the gardener had told the police that Jericho Malone was dead.

"Thank you, Mr. Hubbard," Natalie murmured.

Hubbard's keen eyes darted toward Summerlin. "And you'd be . . . ?"

"Mr. Malone's private secretary," Summerlin answered. "I discovered the—" He glanced uneasily at Natalie, then finished, "The body."

"Well, that ain't strictly true," Longarm put in. "You came in after Mrs. Malone did."

"I came in after she'd killed him," Summerlin said. "So I suppose I was the first innocent person to discover the body."

That second reference was too much for Natalie. She started to sob again.

Hubbard grimaced, glared at Summerlin for a second, then said to the men accompanying him, "Come on, boys. We'd better take a look at the scene and get to work." He led them past Longarm, Natalie, and Summerlin and into the library, then stuck his head back out into the hall to add, "Oh, and nobody leaves the house, all right? I can already see that I'm going to have a lot of questions that need answering before this night is over."

Chapter 4

Longarm shepherded Natalie and Summerlin into the parlor. He lit a couple of lamps and saw that the room was as elegantly and expensively furnished as the rest of the house he had seen so far. Malone hadn't been shy about spending some of the fortune he'd made from his silver mine.

"I don't understand any of this," Natalie complained as she sat down in an armchair. "That detective should go upstairs and arrest Estelle right now. She should be hauled away to prison."

"Prison's where she'd go if she was convicted," Longarm said. "The city jail is where they keep folks who are waiting to come to trial."

"Well, then, he should take her to jail," Natalie insisted. "She belongs behind bars."

Howard Summerlin sat down on a claw-footed divan and clasped his hands together on his rounded belly. "I'm convinced of Estelle's guilt, too, Natalie," he said, "but I suppose these things have to run their course. Do you know that detective well, Marshal?"

"Dan Hubbard?" Longarm said. "Well enough to know he'll do a good job. He ain't fancy, and he goes by the book, but he's all right."

"Wh-what happens next?" Natalie asked. "I can't bear the thought of my father just *lying* in there like that."

"As soon as Dan's finished, he'll send for the undertaker. After that, somebody'll have to make funeral arrangements. Normally, that'd be the widow, but—"

Natalie said coldly, "I won't have her making any arrangements concerning my father. Not ever."

Longarm shrugged. "I reckon it'll be up to you, then, Miss Malone. If you're up to the job."

"I have to be." Natalie squared her shoulders. "That's all I can do for Father now. That, and see to it that his murderer is brought to justice. I can hire the best lawyers—"

Longarm shook his head. "No need for that. If there's a case, the State of Colorado will prosecute it just fine."

"Still, if there's anything I can do, I intend to do it." Natalie's eyes narrowed into hate-filled slits. "I intend to see that witch on the gallows."

Longarm didn't figure it would ever come to that, even if Estelle was charged with Malone's murder and found guilty. If she *had* killed him, it had likely been in the middle of an argument. A jury probably wouldn't condemn her to hang for a crime like that. It was more likely that she would be sentenced to spend the rest of her life in prison.

He hated to think about a woman so young and alive being locked up behind bars for the rest of her life. On the other hand, if Estelle was guilty, she had the punishment coming.

A thought came to him, and he asked, "Did either of you recognize the knife and know where it came from?"

"I . . . I didn't get that good a look at it," Natalie said. Longarm could understand why she hadn't wanted to spend a lot of time studying all the details about the corpse.

Howard Summerlin said, "I recognized it. I've seen it hundreds of times. It belonged to Jericho, and it was usually on his desk. He used it to open letters."

From what Longarm had seen of the weapon, it had struck him as being heavier and thicker than a letter opener. He said, "It looked more like a hunting knife to me."

"Of course," said Summerlin. "That's what it was. But it was the first knife Jericho ever owned, so it had great sentimental value to him. Still, he was efficient enough so that he wanted to get some use out of everything, even something that he kept for sentimental reasons."

That made sense to Longarm. Nobody amassed a fortune like Malone's without being hardheaded and practical.

"What were you doing here this late at night?" he asked Summerlin, giving voice to another question that had occurred to him. "Or do you live here, too?"

Summerlin shook his head. "No, not at all. I have a room in a boardinghouse. But I often stay late, whenever Mr. Malone is working on some papers, as he was tonight."

Longarm took his watch from his vest pocket. It was a gold, turnip-shaped timepiece with a gold chain attached to it. Welded to the other end of that chain and sitting in Longarm's other vest pocket, where it acted as a watch fob, was a two-shot, .41-caliber derringer. Longarm opened the watch now and saw that the hour was after midnight. "Mighty late to be working," he said with a frown.

"Mr. Malone was always one to burn the midnight oil when necessary."

"That's true," Natalie put in. "Father sometimes said he would rather work than sleep."

Longarm grunted. It sounded as if Jericho Malone had had one hell of a work ethic. That was one way to get rich, Longarm supposed, although as a star packer he wouldn't really know. Wealth had never interested him that much, except for the things that it sometimes drove people to do.

He turned his head to look at Natalie. "Were you just

coming in, Miss Malone? Seems like sort of late hours for you, too."

"I was at the Opera House for this evening's presentation of *Hamlet,*" she replied without hesitation. "And after that I had supper with a friend."

Longarm's frown deepened. Natalie's evening had, at least in some respects, duplicated his own.

He wondered if she and her "friend" had also done some of the things he and Maureen had done after supper.

"I reckon people saw you and spoke to you at the Opera House."

"Of course. We sat in Father's regular box. Why are you—" Her eyes suddenly widened with shock and understanding. "My God! You can't seriously think . . . You can't be accusing *me* of having anything to do with—"

Summerlin sat forward angrily. "Good Lord, Marshal, you go too far!" he exclaimed. "I can swear that Miss Malone was out of the house all evening. To accuse her of any sort of complicity in her father's death is preposterous! More than that, it's insane, not to mention insulting!"

"I didn't accuse anybody of anything," Longarm pointed out. "What about you, Summerlin? I know you were here in the house, but where exactly?"

"I have a small office down the hall from the library. Mr. Malone preferred to work in the library itself. I was just going in there to ask him a question about one of the reports we were preparing, when I found . . . when I saw that woman . . ." He broke off his statement and shook his head.

"You don't much cotton to Mrs. Malone, either, do you?"

"As I said before, I considered Mr. Malone to be more than my employer. He was also my friend. And I saw the sort of torments that woman put him through, all because of her baseless fears. There was no excuse for it. No excuse at all."

Longarm finally gave in to the urges that had been

gnawing at him and took out a cheroot. As he was lighting it, a heavy step sounded in the hall, and Dan Hubbard appeared in the entrance to the parlor.

"I've sent for the undertaker, Miss Malone," he said somberly to Natalie. "He should be here soon. In the meantime, there are a few questions I have to ask you."

"More questions?" Natalie said, obviously irritated. "Marshal Long has already been interrogating us."

"Oh, he has, has he?" murmured Hubbard.

Longarm puffed on the cheroot. "Just thinking out loud, more than anything else, Dan."

"No law against that, I suppose," Hubbard said, but clearly he didn't care for the idea that Longarm had questioned the two witnesses before he'd had a chance to. "I've got some questions for you, too, Marshal," Hubbard went on. "But if you and Mr. . . . Summerlin, was it? If the two of you will step out of the parlor, I'd like to talk to Miss Malone privately."

Longarm nodded. "Sure. Come on, Summerlin."

The little man stood up and reluctantly followed Longarm into the hall. Hubbard closed the double doors that led into the parlor. With a frown, Summerlin asked, "Does he have to do that?"

"I reckon he wants to get straight answers from Miss Malone, then ask us the same sort of questions to see if they match up."

"Is all this really necessary? It's obvious what happened."

"Knowin' something is one thing. Provin' it is usually something else."

The clomping sound of more heavy footsteps made them look toward the rear of the mansion. Several men came along the hallway toward the library, led by a rotund man wearing a black suit, white shirt, black string tie, and black top hat. His round, wrinkled face was surprisingly cheery. "In there, boys," he said, pointing into the library. "There's our customer now."

The other men went into the library, carrying a stretcher

and a canvas shroud. Summerlin paled as he watched them troop in, and his pallor grew even deeper a few minutes later when the undertaker and his assistants carried out their grisly, canvas-wrapped burden.

"It shouldn't have happened," he muttered. "It's just not right."

"Murder never is," said Longarm.

It was long after midnight before Hubbard came into the parlor, sat down, placed his hands on his knees, and sighed heavily. From the divan, where he had taken up station earlier, Longarm blew a smoke ring and asked, "Got it all figured out, Dan?"

Hubbard answered the question with one of his own. "Got another of those cheroots?"

Longarm took a cigar from his vest pocket and tossed it over to Hubbard, who caught it, took a small clasp knife from his pocket to trim the end, and lit it with a lucifer. He sat back in the armchair and said, "I hate it when a rich fella gets himself killed. Puts a hell of a lot of pressure on us."

"Are you sayin' you don't try just as hard to solve a murder when the victim don't amount to anything?"

Hubbard's eyes narrowed. "Don't go putting words in my mouth. You know what I mean, Custis. Jericho Malone was friends with the mayor and every other important man in this city. I'll probably hear from all of them tomorrow demanding to know when I'm going to make an arrest."

"Well, let me be the first, then, even though I ain't one of the mucky-mucks. Do you plan to arrest Mrs. Malone?"

Hubbard drew deeply on the cigar, held the smoke for a moment, then exhaled it toward the ceiling. "Looks to me like I have to. Everybody else is accounted for. The daughter was gone for the evening, the servants were in their house out back, and Summerlin was in his office. That just leaves Mrs. Malone."

"You've only got Summerlin's word that he was in his office," Longarm pointed out.

Hubbard waved a hand. "Yeah, but you saw that little weasel. Malone was almost twice his size. You really think he would've just stood there and let Summerlin plant that knife in his chest?"

"Maybe Summerlin took him by surprise."

"Malone fell *in front* of the desk. The knife was kept on top of the desk. Maybe, if Malone had been behind the desk, I would've been able to see how Summerlin could grab up the knife and stab him before he knew what was going on. But the way it was, Summerlin would have had to pick up the knife and then wait for Malone to stand up and come around the desk toward him." Hubbard shook his head. "I just don't see it. If that's the way it was, Malone would have been able to take the knife away from him."

Longarm had already considered all that, even though he had suggested the possibility as a devil's advocate, and he had to admit that Hubbard was right. The only logical suspect in Malone's murder was his wife.

"Where are all of them now?" Longarm asked.

"Mrs. Malone and Miss Malone are upstairs in their rooms. I've got a man guarding each door. I don't want Mrs. Malone getting away—and I don't want Miss Malone getting to her and clawing her eyes out. I sent Summerlin home, and I suppose the cook and the gardener have gone back to bed." Hubbard puffed on the cheroot, then went on, "Why don't you tell me what you saw and how it looks to you, Custis?"

Longarm spent a quarter of an hour doing that. He concluded by saying, "So you see, Dan, I can't tell you who did what. Malone was already dead by the time I got to the library."

"The girl told me that her father and Mrs. Malone had been arguing all day. Summerlin said it went on tonight, even though he and Malone were trying to get some work done."

"What does Mrs. Malone have to say about that?"

"She admits that she and her husband hadn't been getting along. Said that he had a woman he was keeping somewhere, and she didn't like it."

"Malone wanted a divorce, according to his daughter, and Mrs. Malone wouldn't give him one."

Hubbard nodded. "She said she wasn't ready to give up on the marriage. She claims she still loved her husband despite their problems."

"That ain't quite the way Natalie told it. She says her stepmother wouldn't let go 'cause she didn't want Malone getting off that easy."

Hubbard leaned forward in his chair. "Any way you look at it, Custis, it comes up the wife. You know how it is in cases like this. They were fighting, yelling at each other, maybe even struggling. They're standing in front of the desk, she grabs up the knife and stabs him."

"Same thing could've happened with Summerlin," Longarm pointed out. "Since Malone wasn't getting along with his wife, wouldn't it be even harder for her to take him by surprise?"

Hubbard pursed his lips in thought. "Maybe . . . but Malone had his paperwork spread out all over the desk. He was sitting there working on it, say, when Summerlin came in. Why would he get up and go around to the front of the desk? But if it was his wife, he probably *would* stand up so that he could get her out of the room and get back to work." The police detective nodded in satisfaction. "That makes a whole lot more sense to me."

Longarm had to admit that the theory sounded reasonable. Besides, Hubbard was right—in cases like this, it was almost always the spouse who committed the crime.

"I know you're just trying to be fair and look at it from every angle, Custis," Hubbard went on. "And don't go thinking that I've ruled out Summerlin. We'll check into him. But as far as I can see now, he wouldn't have had any reason to kill Malone. He seems to have really looked up to him."

Longarm had gotten that same impression. He tossed the butt of his cheroot into the fireplace, then put his hands on his knees and stood up. "All right, Dan," he said. "I know you'll poke into all the nooks and crannies and come up with the right answer. You need me for anything else?"

Hubbard got to his feet and shook his head. "Can't think of a thing right now." He hesitated, then added, "This was pretty different for you, wasn't it?"

"Bein' just a citizen and a witness instead of a lawman, you mean?" Longarm chuckled. "Yeah. 'Preciate you not pullin' your noose too tight when you found out I'd been talking to Summerlin and Miss Malone."

"Hey, we're on the same side of the fence, aren't we?" Hubbard jerked a thumb toward the door. "Go home and get some sleep. It's late."

Longarm thought about his nine o'clock appointment with Billy Vail and nodded ruefully. And here he had left a warm, willing, redheaded actress in her hotel room bed just so he could get plenty of sleep and arrive at the Federal Building on time.

Those good intentions . . . They'd get a fella every time.

Chapter 5

Jericho Malone's murder hadn't made the front pages of the Denver newspapers, Longarm saw the next morning as he strolled through the lobby of the Federal Building and past the newspaper, shoeshine, and cigar stand. Word of it had probably reached the papers too late to make the morning edition's deadline. Without a doubt, though, the story would be in the day's later editions. Nobody as rich as Malone could die without it being news.

When Longarm walked into the outer office, Henry looked up with a smirk of triumph on his pasty face. "You're late," he told Longarm.

"Only by fifteen minutes."

"Marshal Vail has come out twice to see if you were here yet."

Longarm suppressed a groan. He didn't know why Vail wanted to see him, but the chief marshal's impatience didn't bode well.

Henry's eyes glittered with enjoyment behind his pince-nez glasses. The clerk had a long-standing feud with Longarm, and there was nothing he liked more than seeing the big deputy in trouble with the boss. With relish, he said, "You'd better go on in."

Longarm took off his flat-crowned, snuff-brown Stetson

and tossed it onto the hat tree in the corner. Then he pulled down his vest and marched toward the door leading to Vail's inner office.

"Mornin', Billy," he called as he opened the door and stepped into the room.

From behind the desk, Vail glanced at the banjo clock on the wall and grunted, "Barely."

"Aw, Billy, it's ain't even nine-twenty yet," Longarm said. He closed the door and sat down in the red leather chair in front of Vail's desk.

The chief marshal was pudgy and mostly bald and didn't look much like the hell-roarer he had been in his youth, when he had packed a badge for the Texas Rangers, among other law enforcement organizations. His pale blue eyes were intense as he studied Longarm for a moment; then said, "You look like hell."

Longarm felt like it, too. He had managed to grab only a few hours of sleep. A pot of coffee and a hearty breakfast at the hash house down the street from his rented room had partially restored him, but he was still worn out from the night before.

"Sorry, Billy," he said. "I had a late night—"

"Spare me the lurid details. I saw in the paper that that actress you know is in town with the troupe at the Opera House. I figured you'd be seeing her last night."

"That's only part of it. I sort of stumbled onto a murder."

Vail's eyes widened and he placed his hands palm down on his desk. "Murder?" he repeated. "Who got murdered?"

"Jericho Malone."

For a second, Vail didn't make any response. Then he let out a low whistle of surprise and said, "I hadn't heard about that. Tell me what happened, Custis."

Longarm did so, glad that for a little while, anyway, Vail was distracted from being peeved at him. When he was finished, he said, "I expect Dan Hubbard will arrest Mrs. Malone sometime today."

"You think she did it?"

"I honestly don't know," Longarm replied with a shake of his head. "She looks like the most likely suspect."

Vail gathered up some of the papers on his desk and said, "Well, except for the fact that you'll probably have to be a witness at her trial, it's none of our business. Here, take a look at this." He extended the sheaf of documents across the desk toward Longarm.

Warily, Longarm took the papers and glanced at them. His frown deepened as he flipped through the sheets. "Hell, Billy, I can't make head nor tails of this. It's just a bunch of numbers to me. You'd better have Henry go over it, or find yourself a bookkeeper."

Vail pointed. "Those reports indicate that somebody at one of the Indian agencies up in Montana is either damned incompetent or up to no good. That many supplies don't just go missing and unaccounted for. You're going to head up there and find out what the story is, Custis."

Longarm suppressed a groan. "This is nothing but petty theft, or like you said, pure-dee incompetence. You could get a dozen different deputies to look into this. Why me?"

"The BIA asked for my best man," Vail said as he sat back in his chair and laced his fingers together over his ample belly. "You've worked on dozens of cases that they've sent us, so they know you fit the bill."

Longarm glared down at the documents in his hand, knowing that he was about to spend days, if not weeks, sitting in some stuffy Indian agency office and adding up figures. Ciphering had never been his strong suit. And if somebody *was* robbing Uncle Sam's till, he'd probably wind up getting shot at. Any way you looked at it, this assignment was going to be unpleasant.

"I don't suppose I can talk you out of this," he ventured.

Vail shook his head. "Nope."

Longarm sighed and nodded. "All right," he said. "I reckon Henry's got my travel vouchers?"

"Yep." As Longarm stood up, Vail went on, "You'd

better wrap this up and get back to Denver as quickly as you can, Custis. There's no telling when you'll be needed to testify at Mrs. Malone's trial."

"Assumin' there is a trial."

"Well, sure. But from what you told me about the case, I think it's a pretty sure bet there will be."

Longarm thought so, too. Vail didn't have to worry about him missing the trial, though.

He intended to wrap up that little problem in Montana just as fast as he possibly could.

Longarm was dressed in range clothes and a week's worth of beard stubble on his face when he tromped into Billy Vail's outer office two months later. Henry looked at him and wrinkled his nose. "Aren't there any bathtubs where you've been?" he asked disdainfully.

"Nope," Longarm answered with a jaunty grin, deliberately sounding more cheerful than he felt. In truth, he was tired and dirty and damned glad to be back in civilization. "I had to chase a fella clear to Canada, and there ain't no bathtubs between the Milk River and the border."

"Yes," Henry agreed grudgingly, "we got your wires about being in pursuit of the man who'd been stealing from the Indian agencies. He's in custody, correct?"

"Locked up tight," Longarm said. "And nobody got killed, for a change. You can close the books on this one, Henry."

The clerk jerked a thumb over his shoulder. "Go on in. Marshal Vail is waiting for you."

Longarm went into the inner office. Billy Vail glanced up from his desk and said, "Custis, you look like you've been rode hard and put up wet."

"Feel about that way, too," Longarm said as he slumped into the red leather chair. Now that the door was closed, he didn't have to bother putting on an act for Henry anymore. "This was a rough one, Billy. Come near losin' my hair a couple of times."

Vail nodded. "I know. You did good work. I hated to have to make you hurry back like this."

"I'm glad you did. Your last telegram caught up with me as I was passin' through Cheyenne. If I hadn't got it, I might've been tempted to take a few more days gettin' back."

Vail had a folded newspaper on his desk. He pushed it across to Longarm. "Take a look at that."

Longarm picked up the paper and saw the big headline right away: "TRIAL OF MRS. MALONE TO BEGIN." Smaller headlines read, "Accused Maintains Innocence—Parmalee Confident of Victory in Sensational Case."

"You got out of town at the right time, Custis," Vail said, "or else you'd have been swamped with all the newspaper stories about this case like everybody else in Denver. I never saw such hoopla."

"Folks love to read about a nice juicy murder, I reckon," Longarm mused as he scanned the newspaper article. "It took me so long up north, I was worried the trial would be over before I got back. Who's this Parmalee fella?"

"He's one of the reasons, maybe the main reason, the trial hasn't gotten under way yet. Name's Herbert Parmalee. He's some famous lawyer from back east. Mrs. Malone hired him to defend her, but he couldn't get here for a while because of some other case. He wired Judge Walton and asked for a delay."

Longarm raised his eyebrows and said, "That's a mite unusual, ain't it? I never heard of anybody making a legal motion by telegram."

Vail chuckled. "Creighton didn't like it, that's for sure. He objected up one way and down the other. But Judge Walton decided to give Parmalee the time he asked for. Parmalee blew into town late last week. Trial starts tomorrow."

A grin tugged at the corners of Longarm's mouth. He figured that this Parmalee's delaying tactics had had Abercrombie Creighton, the prosecuting attorney, all lathered up like a hydrophobia skunk. Being a federal lawman, he didn't have a whole lot to do with Creighton, but he knew the man well enough to know he was something of a stuffed shirt, and a windbag to boot. Despite that, Creighton was a good lawyer, with a long record of successful prosecutions.

"I reckon Creighton probably wants to talk to me."

Vail nodded. "He's pestered me and Henry quite a bit about when you'd be back. He's got a copy of the testimony you gave Dan Hubbard, of course, but he'll want to go over it with you before you testify in court."

"I'd go see him now, but I reckon I ought to clean up a mite first."

"That'd be a good idea," Vail said dryly.

Longarm read on down in the newspaper story, which quoted a sorrowful Miss Natalie Malone as hoping that the trial would be a speedy one and that justice would be done. The same sentiment was echoed by Howard Summerlin, Jericho Malone's former private secretary who'd been appointed temporary manager of Malone's business interests.

There were no quotes from Mrs. Estelle Malone, but in an extensive interview, Herbert Parmalee, the noted defense attorney from New York, had stated his certainty that Mrs. Malone would be found innocent once all the facts of the case had been brought to light. "My client is a victim of a series of baseless canards and calumnies," he was quoted as saying.

Longarm said, "Sounds like this fella Parmalee can run ol' Creighton a pretty good race when it comes to spewing hot air."

"He's supposed to be good at what he does," Vail said. "He'll have to be if he hopes to save Mrs. Malone from being convicted."

Longarm tossed the paper back onto the desk. "Well, I'm just as glad I ain't going to be on that jury. All I have to do is get up and tell what I saw, and I can do that."

"You're excused from your duties here for the duration

of the trial. Chances are Creighton will only need you for one day, but he wants to have you handy until it's all over."

"After the past couple of months, I can use a vacation," said Longarm.

Abercrombie Creighton was tall and almost cadaverously thin, with long dark hair and a thin mustache. His eyes were deep-set and piercing, especially when he was staring at witnesses in court and trying to get the truth out of them. His voice was his best feature, deep and sonorous, easily able to reach the back rows of a courtroom. He would have made a good actor, Longarm had often thought, if he hadn't gone into the law instead.

Longarm had had a bath and a shave and splashed on a liberal amount of bay rum. He wore a clean suit of brown tweed, his usual vest, and a snowy white shirt with a black string tie. His boots were the high-topped black ones he always wore, but he'd had them cleaned and shined since getting back to Denver. The hat he held in his left hand had been brushed, too. All in all, by the time he got to Creighton's office in late afternoon, he looked about as respectable as it was possible for him to look.

The prosecuting attorney got up from behind his desk and shook Longarm's hand. "Marshal Long, so good to see you again," he said, his naturally booming voice filling the room. "Please, have a seat."

"Much obliged," Longarm muttered as he sank into an armchair thickly upholstered with black leather.

Creighton settled down behind the desk. "I trust that your mission on behalf of the citizens of our great nation was successfully concluded?"

"Yep, got the miscreant behind bars."

"Excellent, excellent. And Marshal Vail has released you from your duties in his office, as he promised?"

"That's right. I'm all yours until the trial's over, Mr. Creighton."

The attorney laughed. "That shouldn't take long. It's an

open-and-shut case. Mrs. Malone was the only person with both a motive and the opportunity to take her husband's life."

"That we know of," Longarm said with a slight frown.

Creighton blinked in surprise. "What do you mean by that, Marshal? Do you doubt the case against Mrs. Malone?" Creighton started fussing with some of the papers on his desk, shuffling them around as he glared at Longarm. "I'd hate to have to regard a fellow law enforcement professional as a hostile witness . . ."

"That ain't what I mean," Longarm said. "I know it sure looks like Mrs. Malone stabbed her husband. But what about her claim he was already dead when she found him?"

Creighton relaxed and waved a big, long-fingered hand. "What else do you expect the woman to say? Of course she denies her guilt. Most killers insist that they're innocent. But you were there that night and saw her for yourself. No doubt you observed the cold, calculating evil in her eyes for yourself."

"Not really," said Longarm. "She was cryin' most of the time I was around her."

Creighton cleared his throat, clasped his hands together on the desk, and leaned forward. "Be that as it may, I have no doubt of the defendant's guilt. Now, Marshal, if you'll be so kind as to tell me in your own words everything you saw and heard that night . . ."

Longarm repeated his story, going over it just as he had with Dan Hubbard and Billy Vail. Creighton nodded and used a pencil to make notes on a pad as Longarm talked. It didn't take long. When Longarm was finished, Creighton put down his pencil and said, "Very good. Clear, concise testimony, just as I would expect from a veteran lawman such as yourself, Marshal Long. When I call you to the stand, just get up there and tell your story the same way you just told it to me, and there won't be any problems."

"What about this fella Parmalee who's representing

Mrs. Malone? I hear he's supposed to be sharp as a tack. He'll want to cross-examine me, won't he?"

"You don't have to fear Herbert Parmalee, I assure you. The man's reputation is vastly overrated. Just answer his questions truthfully, and I'm sure—"

"Overrated, is it?" The words thundered out in a basso profundo equal to Creighton's own as the door of the prosecuting attorney's office swung open. A short, round man with a white goatee stalked into the room, his face florid with indignation. "We'll see who the jury thinks is overrated!"

"Parmalee!" exclaimed Creighton as he came to his feet. "What the deuce are you doing here? Have you no sense of decorum? Have you no sense of the judicial proprieties?"

"I've forgotten more about judicial proprieties than a stump lawyer like you ever knew, Creighton!"

"Stump lawyer? Why, you pompous popinjay—"

Longarm stopped paying attention as the two lawyers traded long-winded, highfalutin verbal barbs. The old gent with the white goatee was undoubtedly Herbert Parmalee, Estelle Malone's defense attorney.

But at the moment, Longarm was more interested in the pretty gal who had come into Creighton's office behind Parmalee.

Chapter 6

She wore a sober brown traveling outfit that did absolutely nothing for her slender figure. Her dark blond hair was pulled into an unflattering knot on the back of her head and had a matching brown hat perched on it. There was an awkward air about her that reminded Longarm of a colt just learning to walk. She clutched a large leather portfolio to her chest. Overall, she seemed like the sort of young woman to whom Longarm wouldn't give a second glance or even much of a first.

But then he looked at the enormous hazel eyes, the fine-boned, slightly prominent nose, the full-lipped mouth that even devoid of cosmetics had a sensuous appeal to it. The term "diamond in the rough" could have been coined for this young woman.

She glanced at Longarm, then looked away shyly. He grinned as he saw a faint flush rising in her cheeks and on her throat above the tightly buttoned high collar of her dress. His manliness must be more potent than he'd thought, he told himself wryly.

Creighton and Parmalee were still wrangling, their voices growing louder and louder. Since they'd been pretty loud to start with, the charges and countercharges spilled out of the prosecuting attorney's office into the rest of the courthouse. People began to appear in the hallway, drawn by the commotion and curious to see what was going on.

The young woman edged forward and plucked at Parmalee's sleeve. "Father," she said insistently. "Father, please calm down. You know what the doctor said about you getting all worked up."

"Worked up?" Parmalee repeated in a bellow. "I've barely begun demonstrating the deficiencies of this legal charlatan!"

"Get out of my office!" ordered Creighton. "Get out, you grandstanding buffoon! Why, I'll make you rue the day you ever left New York! I'll hang you out to dry! I'll . . . I'll . . ."

This was damned near a historic moment, thought Longarm. Abercrombie Creighton had run out of words.

Well, not quite, he realized a second later as Creighton pointed a quivering finger at Parmalee and said, "Marshal Long, escort this pompous fraud out of my office!"

Longarm, who had avoided Parmalee's wrath so far, got slowly to his feet. As Parmalee turned to glare at him, he thought about reminding Creighton that he worked for the Justice Department and Billy Vail, not the prosecuting attorney's office. But it was too late, because Parmalee had already looked him up and down and now said, "So *this* is the famous Marshal Custis Long! The pistolero with a badge! Rescuer of the downtrodden! Bane of the owlhooter!" Parmalee paused and sneered. "Vilifier of innocent women! Purveyor of false testimony!"

Longarm's eyes narrowed. He said, "Sounds mighty like you're callin' me a liar, old son."

The young woman was pulling urgently on Parmalee's coat by now. "*Father!*" she hissed. "Let's just get out of here! I told you it was a bad idea to come."

Parmalee shook off his daughter's insistent hand and came closer to Longarm. He was so short that he had to tip his head back to glare up into the face of the rangy lawman. Through clenched teeth, he said, "I'm going to destroy you once I get you on the witness stand, Marshal. You know that, don't you?"

Longarm reined in the surge of temper he felt. "I'm just going to get up there and tell the truth, Counselor."

"And when your lies are exposed, will you then draw your revolver and deal out your own brand of justice, as you are so famed for doing?" challenged Parmalee.

"First of all, I ain't what you'd call famous. And second, I don't think Judge Walton allows firearms in his courtroom, so there won't be any hoglegs to pull out."

"Hoglegs!" Parmalee snorted. "My God, sir, you're colorful! I could almost admire a man such as yourself, a sterling example of frontier resourcefulness, were it not for the fact that you willingly place yourself in the service of this . . . this legal buzzard, this eater of judicial carrion, this—"

"Father!" Parmalee's daughter shouted at him.

Blinking, the defense attorney fell silent. He was breathing hard, and his face was brick-red. But the hostile glare he directed at Longarm and Creighton had lost none of its power. Several seconds passed in strained silence, then Parmalee tugged down his coat and cleared his throat. "I came here to make one final request that the ridiculous charge against my client be dismissed," he said.

"Denied," Creighton said coldly.

"Very well, then. I shall see you in court." Parmalee glanced at Longarm, said "Hmmph!" and turned away. "Come along, Janice."

"Father, you can't let yourself get carried away like that," the young woman said to him as they went out of the office. "You know what the doctor said . . ."

Several men came hurrying up to Parmalee and his daughter, surrounding them and closing them off from sight as they went on down the corridor. Longarm recognized them as reporters for the Denver papers.

"The nerve of that old fraud!" Creighton said. "He only did this to draw attention to himself and get his name in the newspapers again. He knew good and well I wasn't going to dismiss the murder charge against Mrs. Malone."

Longarm nodded. "I suspect you're right."

"Well, now you've seen for yourself the quality of our opposition, Marshal. You can understand why I'm confident of a conviction. Parmalee has no chance."

"The papers made it sound like he's got a pretty good reputation back East."

"His successes have been very much blown out of proportion, I assure you." Creighton took a long, thick cigar from a humidor on his desk and began trimming it with a small knife with a gold-plated handle. "I'm glad we didn't have to resort to force to get him to leave. The so-called journalists in this town would have surely distorted the facts of such a confrontation. Cigar?"

"No, thanks," Longarm said. "I got my own. Three for a nickel."

Creighton grimaced.

"Who was the gal?" Longarm asked.

"What? Oh, you mean the young woman with Parmalee. His daughter, I believe."

"Figured that much, since she kept calling him Father."

Creighton's jaw tightened at what he probably took to be insolence. "Evidently she functions as his clerk and assistant. You saw her for yourself . . . drab, mousy little thing . . . Can't attract a man so she devotes herself to work instead." Creighton lit the cigar and puffed on it. "If ever a female was born to be an old maid, young Miss Parmalee is that woman."

Remembering her eyes and mouth, Longarm wasn't so sure about that. He wasn't looking forward to the trial of Estelle Malone, other than being anxious to get it over with . . .

But he found himself more than willing to have another look at Janice Parmalee.

Not surprisingly, the first day of the trial drew quite a crowd. Longarm wasn't sure he had ever seen quite so many people around the courthouse. Tall and broad-shouldered as he was, he was able to make his way through the press of reporters and spectators. He ran into Abercrombie Creighton just outside the door of Judge Angus Walton's courtroom, and the prosecuting attorney gripped Longarm's hand tightly.

Creighton leaned his head close to Longarm's and said, "I'll be calling Howard Summerlin first, then the servants, then you, Marshal. I hope to get you on the stand this afternoon." Creighton had lost all his fancy rhetoric. Now he was all business. The flowery talk would come back once the trial started, Longarm was sure, but there was no need for it here in the corridor.

"I'll be ready," Longarm told the prosecuting attorney. He looked around, hoping to catch a glimpse of Janice Parmalee.

Instead he saw the crowd part to let Natalie Malone and Howard Summerlin through to the courtroom. Natalie wore a black dress with a black, gauzy veil over her face and looked lovely despite being in mourning. Summerlin ushered her along with a solicitous hand on her arm.

They paused to greet Longarm and Creighton. "Hello, Marshal," Natalie said with a solemn nod to Longarm. She looked completely different from the wild-eyed, grief-stricken, furious young woman she had been the last time Longarm saw her. Today she was calm and reserved.

Summerlin seemed as nervous as ever. He gave Longarm a curt "Marshal," then said to Natalie, "We'd better get inside. I don't like crowds."

She went with him without protest. Longarm frowned a little. It looked like Summerlin was pulling Natalie's strings now. Well, that wasn't too surprising, Longarm told himself. Summerlin was taking care of all the business affairs. It was only natural that Natalie would come to lean on him, at least to a certain extent.

Longarm wondered idly if Summerlin had any hopes of taking that arrangement to a completely different level.

A burst of noise made him turn his head and look the other way down the corridor. Estelle Malone was being escorted by a pair of uniformed guards toward the courtroom. She wore a plain gray dress that Longarm knew was jail issue. Her ash-blond hair was neatly brushed, however, and her face, though pale, was composed. She wasn't wearing handcuffs. Following her and the guards came Herbert Parmalee, and Janice brought up the rear of the small group. They all turned and disappeared into a side hallway before they reached the main door of the courtroom. Longarm knew the guards would take Estelle into the courtroom through a side entrance.

Creighton said, "Take a seat anywhere inside, Marshal. I'll call you when I'm ready."

Longarm nodded and followed Creighton into the courtroom. Estelle and the Parmalees were already at the defense table, on the left side of the room facing the judge's bench. Creighton went to the prosecution table on the other side. A brightly polished wooden railing divided the room, with the seats for the spectators and witnesses behind it. Summerlin and Natalie were already seated, but all the other chairs were empty. The guards at the door weren't letting the spectators and reporters in yet. Longarm took a seat in the back row of the courtroom.

A man and a woman came in a few minutes later. Longarm recognized the man as the gardener from the Malone estate, who had gone to fetch the police on the night of the murder. The middle-aged woman with him had to be his wife, who worked as the cook and housekeeper for the Malone family. Their name was Carlson, Longarm recalled.

Daniel Hubbard walked in next. He gave Longarm a friendly nod and sat down on the front row, a few chairs away from Summerlin and Natalie. He balanced his derby on his knee.

Soon after that, the doors were opened to the public, and the courtroom filled up in a hurry. The noise in the room rose. Everyone had an opinion on a notorious case like this, and nobody seemed to be shy about sharing it. Longarm wished he could smoke. A drink of Maryland rye would have gone down even better. He sat there and tried not to fidget too much.

Court was supposed to convene at nine o'clock. Longarm took out his watch and checked the time. Only a few more minutes, he saw. He snapped the watch closed and replaced it in his vest pocket. The comforting weight of the .41 derringer rode in his other vest pocket. He hadn't worn his Colt today, knowing that it wouldn't be allowed in the courtroom. But nobody had asked him if he had a derringer in his pocket, and he hadn't been searched. The likelihood of needing a gun was pretty slim, but Longarm felt better knowing he wasn't completely unarmed.

Finally, in his loud Irish brogue, the bailiff shouted, "All rise!" and all in the courtroom came to their feet. Silence settled down over the crowd as Judge Angus Walton came out of his chambers and walked to the bench. Longarm knew Judge Walton pretty well. He was a small, birdlike man with a sour temper and a pair of the bushiest eyebrows Longarm had ever seen on a human being. He knew the law backward and forward and applied it evenhandedly, which was about the highest praise a judge could be given, in Longarm's opinion.

Walton stepped up to his chair, sat down with a rustle of black robes, and picked up his gavel. He banged it once and said, "Court's in session. Everybody sit down. Bailiff, bring in the jury."

The bailiff did so, opening the door to the jury room and crooking his finger. A dozen men came out and took their seats in the jury box. The jury had been selected the day before, Longarm recalled reading in the paper. He scanned their faces but didn't see anybody he knew. Most of them were townies, but three of the jury members were cowboys. Longarm recognized them by their scrubbed, sunburned faces and their clean but well-worn range clothes. All of the jurymen looked solemn. They were taking this mighty seriously, and that was good.

"The clerk will read the charge," Judge Walton instructed.

The clerk stood up and read off a paper in his hand. "Case four-eighteen . . . the State of Colorado versus Mrs. Estelle Malone . . . The charge is murder."

From where he sat, Longarm couldn't see Estelle's face, but he saw a tiny shiver go through her at the sound of the words.

"The defendant has entered a plea of not guilty," Walton said as the clerk sat down. "Is there any change in that plea?"

Herbert Parmalee got to his feet. "No, Your Honor. The defendant still maintains her innocence."

Walton looked at Abercrombie Creighton. "Is the prosecution ready?"

Creighton stood up as well. "Yes, Your Honor."

"Defense counsel is ready?"

Parmalee said, "Yes, Your Honor."

"Very well." Walton sat back in his chair. "Mr. Creighton, I'll hear your opening statement."

"Thank you, Your Honor," Creighton said as Parmalee sat down next to Estelle. The prosecuting attorney came out from behind his table and clasped his hands behind his back as he began to speak. "Your Honor, gentlemen of the jury, distinguished guests of the court . . . the prosecution in this case will prove beyond a shadow of a doubt that the defendant, Mrs. Estelle Malone, did intentionally and willfully, with a very great deal of malice aforethought indeed, murder her husband, the illustrious financier and silver magnate, the esteemed Mr. Jericho Malone, by cold-bloodedly plunging a knife into his chest! She was a veritable viper in the bosom of this great man, who was struck down heinously in the prime of his life, callously taken from his loving daughter and his many, many friends, with no other reason than the sheer, spiteful hatred of a wicked, wicked woman!" Creighton's voice thundered as he spun around sharply and pointed an accusing finger at Estelle Malone.

He went on like that for a good fifteen minutes, praising Jericho Malone and damning Estelle with all the fervor of a hellfire-and-brimstone backwoods preacher. Longarm watched the crowd eating it up, and then, just as the spectators began to tire of Creighton's harangue, the prosecuting attorney sensed it and reached a thunderous climax, concluding, "And thus, justice will be served!" He struck a noble pose for a couple of seconds, then stalked back to his table and sat down.

Into the sudden silence that sounded a little odd after all that yelling, Judge Walton turned to Parmalee and said, "Counselor?"

Longarm had been watching Creighton's theatrics, so he was a little surprised when he looked at Parmalee and saw that the defense attorney was hunched forward over the table. Parmalee put his hands on the table, however, and pushed himself to his feet. He straightened and walked out from behind the table. When he turned so that Longarm could see his profile, Longarm was shocked to see how flushed Parmalee's face was.

Janice was worried, Longarm saw as he glanced at her. She was leaning forward tensely, her eyes fixed on her father.

Parmalee's voice was strong as he began in ringing tones, "My learned colleague has spoken much of justice here this morning. What sort of justice is it when an innocent woman is charged and brought to trial for a crime she did not commit?" Parmalee lifted a clenched fist. "It is a travesty of justice! A travesty, I tell you!" He pointed at Estelle, much as Creighton had done earlier. "This woman . . . this poor, bereaved widow who has lost the man she loved above all else in this world . . . this woman who is denied the basic human dignity of being allowed to wear her own clothing but who is instead paraded before a gawking mass of spectators in prison drab . . . this woman who wants only to grieve for the beloved husband who was taken from her so violently . . . this woman is innocent, I say! Innocent!" Parmalee pounded his fist into the palm of his other hand. "Innocent! Inn . . . Inn . . ."

Suddenly, his booming voice faltered. He took a stumbling step forward and shook his head. "Inn . . . ocent," he croaked. He turned slowly toward the jury box, and from that angle Longarm could see his face. Parmalee's features were twisted in pain. The fist he had been pounding into his other hand was now pressed against his chest.

Judge Walton leaned forward, an anxious frown on his lined face. "Counsel? Mr. Parmalee? Are you all right?"

Janice Parmalee was on her feet. "Father!" she screamed.

Parmalee turned one more time, muttered, "Innocent," then pitched forward onto his face.

Chapter 7

Longarm surged to his feet as chaos filled the courtroom. Nearly everyone was standing up now, and people were shouting questions. Longarm's height allowed him to see over the heads of many of the spectators, and he saw Janice Parmalee leave her seat at the defense table and rush across the courtroom toward her fallen father.

Judge Walton banged hard on the bench with his gavel, each sharp crack of the wooden instrument sounding like a gunshot. "Order!" Walton bellowed in a voice that seemed too big for his frail body. "I'll have order in this courtroom, blast it! Order!"

No one was paying any attention to the judge. Herbert Parmalee's collapse had created too much of a sensation. The reporters and the rest of the spectators pressed forward, eager to see what was going on. Even Abercrombie Creighton was staring.

Longarm couldn't see Janice anymore. She must be kneeling beside her father, he thought. But he heard her clearly enough as she cried, "Oh, God, help him! Can't somebody help him? Father!"

There was one sure way of quieting down a commotion. Longarm reached into his vest pocket, slipped out the derringer, and fired one of the barrels into the ceiling.

The banging of Judge Walton's gavel might have scunded like gunshots, but this was the real thing and everyone in the room realized it. A sudden silence fell, and heads swiveled around as people looked for the source of the shot.

Longarm dropped the derringer back in his vest pocket and strode forward, bulling his way through the crowd to the railing and slapping open the gate in it. He could see Janice now. She was on her knees next to the crumpled shape of her father, just as Longarm had thought. She looked up at him with a pale, tear-streaked face and said in a small voice, "Can't someone please help?"

Longarm's voice rang out, filling the room just as Creighton's and Parmalee's had earlier. "We need a sawbones up here," he said. "Any doctors in the court?"

Dan Hubbard came up beside him. "I don't think you're going to find a doctor in here, Custis, but I'll send for one."

"Make it fast," Longarm muttered, then moved over to kneel beside Parmalee, on the other side of his body from Janice.

Longarm put a couple of fingers to Parmalee's neck and felt for a pulse. After a second, he located it, fast and irregular but definitely there. "He's alive, ma'am," he said to Janice, "and a doctor should be on the way real soon."

"He shouldn't have gotten so worked up . . . The doctor warned him . . . said the trip could be dangerous . . . had to take it easy . . ."

Janice was babbling, but despite that Longarm had a pretty good idea what she was getting at. "He's got a bad heart, don't he?"

She looked at him and nodded. "Can't you *do* anything?"

"I'm sorry, Miss Parmalee, but I ain't a medical man."

Judge Walton had given up on restoring order. He came down from the bench and hurried over to join Longarm and Janice beside Parmalee. Abercrombie Creighton had come up behind Longarm and was peering curiously over the lawman's shoulder.

"What's wrong with him?" Walton demanded.

Longarm saw Janice flinch at the brusqueness of the judge's tone. He said, "Bad ticker, Your Honor."

"Oh. I'm sorry to hear that. Suppose I'll have to declare a recess."

"The State will raise no objection to that, Your Honor," Creighton said.

"Hmmph. Big of you." Walton looked around and spotted the bailiff. "Have the defendant taken back to jail," the judge ordered. "And clear the courtroom. We stand in recess. Everybody vamoose!"

It took all the officers that could be summoned from elsewhere in the courthouse, but eventually all the spectators had been prodded out of the courtroom. A couple of minutes later, Dan Hubbard came in with a gray-haired man carrying a black medical bag. Longarm stood up and moved back a few steps to give the doctor some room. The medico knelt beside Parmalee and gently rolled the collapsed attorney onto his back. He loosened Parmalee's collar and unbuttoned his vest and shirt, then took a stethoscope from his bag and began listening to the lawyer's heart.

Creighton said to Walton, "Your Honor, what effect is this unfortunate development going to have on the trial?"

"We're in recess," snapped Walton. "Don't talk to me about the trial out of chambers. That's where I'm going now. But don't take that as an invitation, Creighton!"

Walton stalked out of the courtroom, vanishing through the door to the left of the bench. Creighton frowned after him.

Natalie Malone and Howard Summerlin had been allowed to remain in the courtroom. They came up to Creighton, and Natalie asked, "There's still going to be a trial, isn't there, Mr. Creighton?"

"Of course," replied the prosecuting attorney. "There may be a delay, but—"

"Another delay?" Summerlin broke in. "My God, hasn't justice been delayed long enough already?"

Longarm frowned. He didn't much like the idea of this legal wrangling going on while only a few feet away the doctor was examining Herbert Parmalee to see if he was going to live. Janice still knelt beside her father. She had taken hold of one of his hands, and her tear-filled eyes were fixed on his face. Her lips moved silently. Longarm figured she was praying.

He put his hand on Creighton's arm and said quietly, "Let's give these folks some breathing room, why don't we?"

Creighton hesitated. He was pompous and arrogant but not totally without sympathy for his fallen opponent. He nodded and said, "Of course. Miss Malone, Mr. Summerlin, please come with me."

He ushered them out of the now nearly empty courtroom. Longarm thought that he ought to go, too, since he didn't have any official connection with the Parmalees, but something kept him there. That something, he realized, was Janice. He was unwilling to leave her alone with her father and the doctor. He didn't know her, had barely exchanged a dozen words with her, but still he felt compelled to stay.

After a few minutes, when the doctor had finished his examination of Parmalee, he looked up at Janice and said, "This man will have to be taken to the hospital immediately. He's suffered a serious heart seizure."

"Will . . . will he live?" Janice asked.

"I couldn't tell you that, miss. I'll do everything I can for him. You're his daughter, is that correct?"

Janice swallowed hard and nodded.

"Any other relatives here in Denver?"

This time she shook her head. "We're from . . . from New York."

"All right. You'll have to come to the hospital with him. I sent for an ambulance wagon before I even arrived here at the courthouse, so it should be arriving soon."

"Th-thank you." Janice drew a deep breath. "Please save him."

The doctor permitted himself a slight smile. "I'll certainly try, miss."

A couple of minutes later, two men hurried into the courtroom carrying a stretcher. Longarm stepped up beside Janice, who was still kneeling next to her father, and lightly touched her shoulder. "Better step back, Miss Parmalee," he murmured.

She came to her feet, and he put a hand under her elbow to help her as she straightened. "Thank you. You're Marshal Long, aren't you?"

"That's right, ma'am. Custis Long. Anything I can do to help you, you just let me know."

Janice turned her hazel eyes on him. "We're on opposite sides of this case, though."

"I don't reckon anybody's too worried about that at a time like this."

"Thank you, Marshal. Thank you for . . . for taking charge of things earlier."

The ambulance attendants loaded Herbert Parmalee onto the stretcher and fastened broad leather straps over his body so that he couldn't roll off. They picked up the stretcher and carried it out of the courtroom. The doctor followed closely behind them. Janice and Longarm brought up the rear of the little procession. Guards cleared a path through the curious crowd in the lobby of the courthouse, so that the attendants were able to carry Parmalee out of the building and place him in the back of the ambulance wagon that was waiting outside. The doctor motioned for Janice to come with him and got into the back of the wagon. The attendants climbed onto the seat in front, where one of them took up the reins of the four-horse team hitched to the ambulance.

Longarm watched from the steps of the courthouse as the driver flapped the reins and got the team moving. As the wagon rolled away down the street, Abercrombie Creighton came up beside Longarm and said, "Judge Walton's clerk just told me that the judge is calling the court back into session at eleven o'clock."

Longarm looked over sharply at the prosecuting attorney. "How can he do that? Mrs. Malone's lawyer is in that ambulance, on his way to the hospital."

"Perhaps he's going to declare a mistrial." Creighton shook his head. "I hope not. As Miss Malone and Mr. Summerlin said, there have already been enough delays in this proceeding."

"You can't have a trial without a defense attorney," Longarm pointed out.

"There are other lawyers here in Denver. Plenty of them, in fact. I'm sure Mrs. Malone can find someone else to represent her in short order."

Longarm frowned. He didn't have any strong opinions on the case, other than that it looked like Estelle Malone was probably guilty, but it didn't seem fair to him that the defendant might have to find another lawyer in a hurry, a lawyer who might not be as talented as Herbert Parmalee. Still, the wheels of justice had to grind on at their own pace. He was just a witness, after all, and nobody was going ask for his opinion on legal matters.

"I just wanted to let you know," Creighton went on, "so that you won't leave the vicinity."

"You don't reckon I'll be testifying today, do you?"

Creighton laughed. "The way this case is going, Marshal, I don't really have any idea *what* to expect next!"

Instead of subduing the crowd, the collapse of Herbert Parmalee had the opposite effect. When the spectators filled Judge Walton's courtroom again just before eleven o'clock, the hubbub was even louder than it had been before. Everyone was buzzing about what had happened to Parmalee, wondering what was going on at the hospital, and speculating on what the judge would do next.

Longarm sat in the front row of the spectators' section this time, so that in case anything else bizarre happened, he wouldn't have to force his way through the crowd as he'd done before. He looked at the defense table. Estelle Malone sat there alone, having been brought in by her guards a few minutes earlier. She looked lost and confused, and Longarm felt a twinge of sympathy for her. If she really was innocent, she had to be wondering what was going to happen to her now.

At straight-up eleven o'clock, the bailiff called out for everyone to rise. They did so as Judge Walton came into the courtroom and took his seat at the bench. He smacked down his gavel and growled, "Sit down. Court is now once again in session."

Abercrombie Creighton was on his feet immediately. "Your Honor?"

"What is it, Counsel?"

"In light of the events of earlier this morning, the State moves for an adjournment until nine o'clock tomorrow."

Longarm watched as Estelle Malone looked around dazedly, as if uncomprehending of what all this meant.

Judge Walton pursed his lips and said, "Denied."

Creighton blinked. "Your Honor? I'm afraid I don't understand—"

"The State's motion is denied, Mr. Creighton. I can't make it any plainer than that."

"Your Honor, in the opinion of the prosecution, a mistrial under these circumstances is uncalled for. A continuance, perhaps—"

Again Walton interrupted. "Who said anything about a mistrial? I'm going to adjourn this court until one o'clock this afternoon, at which time the case will resume."

Creighton looked flabbergasted, and judging by the buzz that went through the courtroom, everyone else felt the same way.

Estelle Malone's pallor had deepened, Longarm noted. She was probably figuring out what the judge's words meant to her and her defense.

As Walton gaveled for quiet, Estelle rose shakily to her feet. "Your Honor?" she said.

"Yes, Mrs. Malone?"

"I . . . I don't have a lawyer."

"There are many competent attorneys in Denver, madam. You have until one o'clock to retain one of them and acquaint him with the facts of your case."

"But, Your Honor . . . with all due respect . . . that's not enough time—"

Walton leaned forward and said sharply, "Mrs. Malone, I regret the unfortunate fact that Mr. Parmalee was stricken. However, I have already granted lengthy delays in this case, and any more would seriously compromise the right of both the defendant *and the State* to a speedy trial. I will not postpone this trial any longer. Given the unusual circumstances, however, I hereby order that you be released from custody—to remain under close guard and supervision, however—so that you may meet with whichever attorney you choose to represent you and agree to terms with him. I am confident that you can reach an arrangement with a new attorney and that he can be prepared for trial by one o'clock."

That was damned near the most outrageous thing Longarm had ever heard in a courtroom, and his opinion of Judge Walton slipped a notch. He hadn't expected the judge to be so arbitrary and heavy-handed. Abercrombie Creighton looked surprised, too. The prosecuting attorney wasn't raising any objections to Judge Walton's decision, however. With less than two hours to prepare a defense, any lawyer Estelle might choose, no matter how skilled, would be hopelessly outmatched by Creighton.

"Your Honor," Estelle said desperately, "I can't—"

"You have no choice in the matter, Mrs. Malone." Walton reached for his gavel to signal the adjournment. "Court will resume at one—"

"Your Honor!" The voice came from the back of the courtroom, and it was barely strong enough to be heard over the commotion. The speaker tried again. "Your Honor, please!"

Walton held the gavel upright, poised to strike. "Eh? What is it?"

Longarm turned his head and saw an unexpected figure stride forward to the gate in the railing. Janice Parmalee opened the gate, walked through it, and went over to the defense table. An anticipatory silence settled down over the courtroom as she patted Estelle Malone on the shoulder, then took off her drab brown hat and placed it on the table. She turned back toward the bench, and her chin lifted as she said, “Janice Parmalee for the defense, Your Honor. We’ll be ready when court resumes at one o’clock.”

Chapter 8

The gavel rapped sharply on the bench, but instead of beginning the adjournment, it signified Judge Walton once again trying to restore order in the courtroom. Janice's announcement had been followed by a second of stunned silence that had then erupted into noise.

"Objection, Your Honor!" Creighton shouted. "The defendant must be represented by qualified counsel, otherwise this trial will be naught but a mockery of the dignified legal proceeding it should be."

Janice's eyes flashed daggers as they glanced toward Creighton's tall, lean figure. Then she turned back to the judge and said in a loud, clear voice, "Your Honor, I am fully qualified to represent my client in this matter. I am a member in good standing of the New York State Bar Association and will be happy to furnish my credentials if it would please the court."

Walton glared back and forth between Janice and Creighton for a moment, then said, "It would please the court if both counsels would approach the bench."

They did so, and Walton leaned forward to talk to them. Longarm strained his ears, but even his keen hearing couldn't pick up what was being said. He was grinning anyway. Seeing both Judge Walton and Abercrombie

Creighton dumbfounded that way had been downright enjoyable.

The judge shooed Janice and Creighton away from the bench, and they went back to their respective sides of the courtroom. With his eyes slitted and angry, Walton said, "As in the case of her father, the court acknowledges and accepts the judgment of the New York State Bar Association that Miss Janice Parmalee is qualified to practice the noble profession of law. Miss Parmalee, is it your contention that you are familiar with the particulars of this case?"

"It is, Your Honor," Janice said. "I helped my father prepare his defense of Mrs. Malone and I am fully aware of the details of the case, more so than any other attorney who might be hired by my client."

"Mrs. Malone." Walton looked at Estelle. "Is it your wish to be represented by Miss Parmalee?"

Estelle looked at Janice like someone who had just thrown her a rope as she was sinking in quicksand. "Yes, Your Honor," she said.

Creighton said, "Your Honor, this is highly irregular—"

"Unusual, yes, but irregular, no," Walton snapped. "Women are allowed by the statutes of this state to practice law. The fact that few of them do in no abrogates their right to do so."

"Of course, Your Honor," Creighton said smoothly. "It is just that sometimes the work of the legal profession is harsh and unpleasant, and as a gentleman, it is my wish to spare the fair flower of womanhood from such harshness and unpleasantness—"

"Your Honor," Janice broke in, "with all due respect to the gentleman, if my hands get a bit dirty, I'm fully capable of washing them."

Longarm burst out with a bray of laughter. He wasn't the only one. An uproar of hilarity filled the courtroom until Walton hammered it down with his gavel.

"Marshal!" the judge said scathingly, selecting Longarm as the easiest target. "Please control yourself, or I'll find you in contempt of court. I'm already extremely peeved at you for discharging a firearm in my courtroom."

"I'm sorry, Your Honor," Longarm said, still grinning. "I'll keep it reined in."

"You do that." Walton turned back to Creighton, who was glaring at Longarm. "Now, Counselor, if you have an actual legal objection, rather than a chivalric one . . ."

"No, Your Honor." Creighton forced out the words. "The State has no objection to Miss Parmalee serving as counsel for the defense."

"Very well. If we're finally done . . . ?" Walton raised the gavel, paused, then brought it down. "Court is adjourned until one o'clock!"

Naturally, the reporters clustered around Janice Parmalee, shouting questions and scribbling on their pads. Despite the calm strength she had shown in confronting Judge Walton and Abercrombie Creighton a few minutes earlier, the journalistic badgering quickly made her look nervous, Longarm thought. He gave the reporters a little time to ask their questions, then moved up among them and said sternly, "You fellas better give the lady a chance to catch her breath. Besides, I reckon she's got work to do."

Janice gave him an appreciative glance, then said to the journalists, "I really have to consult with my client, gentlemen." She picked up the leather portfolio she had carried into court earlier that morning, when she had been meekly following her father rather than leading the way herself. "If you'll excuse me . . ."

Creighton came shouldering through the press of people around Janice. "Miss Parmalee," he said stiffly. "I'd like to inquire as to the condition of your father."

"He is resting at the hospital and, according to the doctor, doing as well as can be expected following his seizure," Janice said. "Thank you, Counsel, for your solicitude."

Creighton inclined his head and looked grave. "I wish him only the best, of course."

Longarm would have stayed there with Janice, but Creighton took hold of his arm and tugged him away. Longarm thought about resisting knowing that a skinny gent like Creighton couldn't budge him if he didn't want to go, but he decided it would be better to go along for now.

As they left the courtroom, Creighton hissed, "You've played the gallant protector quite enough with Miss Parmalee, Marshal. Have you forgotten that you're a witness for the prosecution, not the defense?"

"I was just tryin' to be a gentlemen," Longarm said coldly. "Seems I recollect somebody else spoutin' sentiments like that not long ago."

"Yes, well, I haven't forgotten how amused you were by Miss Parmalee's retort, either." Creighton stopped and frowned in thought. "I understand how you feel, Marshal. Miss Parmalee *is* female, though not the fairest example of the species."

"She might surprise you about that," Longarm said, thinking of the unplumbed depths he had glimpsed in Janice's eyes.

"Be that as it may, you have to check any sympathetic impulses you may be feeling. The defendant is still guilty of murder, no matter what the sex of her attorney."

"Guilt ain't been proved yet, and I seem to recollect something about a defendant being innocent until proved guilty."

Creighton waved that off. "Yes, yes, of course. And I want to be fair, Marshal. You saw that for yourself. I objected when Judge Walton said he was going to proceed with the trial this afternoon."

Longarm shrugged. "At first. Then you got to liking the idea."

Through gritted teeth, Creighton said, "I'm not going to have this argument with you, Marshal. All I'm saying is that you had better not compromise my prosecution of this case out of the misguided sense that you're some sort of knight errant who has to rescue Miss Parmalee. If you do, you'll be leaving yourself open to charges of obstructing justice."

"You just do your job, Creighton," Longarm snapped. "I'll get up there and tell the truth, just like I've said all along."

He turned on his heel and walked away. He wanted a drink, a steak, and a smoke, in that order, and he only had until one o'clock to round them up.

Longarm was a little later than he'd intended to be getting back to the courtroom, but things hadn't gotten under way when he came in the door. But his tardiness had cost him a place to sit, he saw as he glanced around. Every chair and bench in the place was full. He joined the row of reporters who were standing up in the rear of the room. Taking off his hat, he leaned his broad shoulders against the wall.

Creighton was at the prosecution table, and sitting next to him was a man in a sober suit and spectacles. Probably a clerk or another lawyer who would take notes during the trial. Over at the defense table, Janice Parmalee didn't have anyone to help her. She sat with Estelle Malone, the two women alone at the table. They were talking quietly. Janice tried to smile and look reassuring, but Longarm wasn't sure she carried it off. Estelle patted her hand, almost as if the older woman were comforting the younger, instead of the other way around.

A couple of minutes later, Judge Walton came in. Longarm was already on his feet, so he didn't have to rise. But he didn't get to sit down when the judge did, either. Walton rapped the gavel and said, "Court is now in session. Miss Parmalee, your father was in the middle of his opening statement when he was, ah, stricken by his illness. Would you care to continue?"

Janice stood up and nodded. "Yes, Your Honor." She turned and walked toward the jury box. Longarm thought she looked a mite scared, but she was controlling it well. She came to a stop in front of the jury and said, "Gentlemen." In contrast to the booming tones of her father and Abercrombie Creighton, Janice's voice was quiet. Several of the jury members even leaned forward in order to hear her better. "I'm afraid I don't share my father's oratorical skills, nor can I rival Mr. Creighton's eloquence. But I can tell you this: My client, Mrs. Estelle Malone, is innocent of the crime with which she is charged. She loved her husband, despite any troubles they might have had. She would never have taken his life. I believe that, and I intend to prove it to you, too. Thank you."

Longarm nodded a little, approvingly, as Janice turned and walked back to the defense table. Her statement had been short, simple, and to the point. It seemed even more so when compared to Creighton's bombast and bluster. Longarm had a pretty good idea Janice knew what she was doing by making the jurymen draw that same comparison.

At the prosecution table, Creighton was glowering. He knew he had been upstaged. He forced that expression off his face as Judge Walton said to him, "Proceed, Counselor."

Creighton came to his feet. "Yes, Your Honor. The State calls Howard Summerlin."

Summerlin stood up from his chair and stepped forward. He put his hand on the Bible and was sworn in, then took the seat to Judge Walton's left, between the bench and the jury box. Abercrombie Creighton began the questioning by asking him his occupation.

"Before his tragic death, I was private secretary to Mr. Jericho Malone," Summerlin said. "At present, I am managing the business affairs of Mr. Malone's estate on behalf of his daughter."

"So, while he was alive, you worked closely with Mr. Malone?"

"Yes, I did. I saw him practically every day, often working side by side with him for hours at a time. I like to think that we were . . . friends . . . as well as employer and employee."

"You regarded his death as a personal blow?"

"Of course. I was very upset when he was murdered."

Janice rose to her feet. "Objection, Your Honor. It has not been established in evidence that Jericho Malone was murdered."

Walton frowned at her and said, "You don't think he stabbed himself in the chest, do you?" Before Janice could reply, the judge grimaced and went on, "You're right, though, Counsel. Mr. Creighton, you've not yet laid the proper groundwork for the witness to answer the question in that matter. The objection is sustained, and the witness is instructed to answer only in terms of his own personal knowledge."

"Permit me to clarify, Your Honor," Creighton murmured. "Mr. Summerlin, you meant to say that you were very upset at Mr. Malone's death, didn't you?"

"Yes, that's right," Summerlin said, but the glare directed at Estelle Malone left no one in the courtroom unaware that he had meant what he said the first time around.

"Tell us, then, what you witnessed on the night in question and know to be true of your own personal knowledge."

"Certainly." Summerlin hitched himself forward a little in the witness chair. "Mr. Malone and I were working at his house, preparing some reports for the minority stockholders in the Colorado Star."

"The Colorado Star being . . . ?" Creighton prompted.

"The silver mine that Mr. Malone owns . . . owned. It's the primary source of his fortune, though he also had investments in banking, business, and real estate, all funded by the mine. There are several minority stockholders in Mr. Malone's ventures, but he holds . . . held the majority of all stock."

"Were you and Mr. Malone working in the same room?"

Summerlin shook his head. "No, I have a small office down the hall from the library. That was where Jericho preferred to work. I was in my office, late in the evening, when a question came up that I needed Mr. Malone to answer."

"When you say late in the evening, when precisely do you mean?"

"I don't know the exact time," Summerlin said. "But I know it was late, probably close to midnight."

"Were you accustomed to staying that late at Mr. Malone's house?"

"When we were working, yes. Mr. Malone liked to work at night, and besides, he hadn't gotten much work done that day because he'd been fighting with his wife."

The legs of Janice's chair made a slight scraping sound as she started to get up, but Creighton forestalled her objection by saying quickly, "You know this of your own personal knowledge, Mr. Summerlin?"

"I should say so," Summerlin replied. "I was there most of the day and heard them shouting at each other."

Longarm saw Janice relax in her chair. Creighton had effectively blocked her from objecting to the testimony about the trouble between Jericho and Estelle Malone.

"These . . . domestic disagreements, if you will . . . did many of them take place in the Malone household?"

"Frequently."

"And in your opinion, who instigated these shouting matches?"

Summerlin looked directly at Estelle once more. "Mrs. Malone."

"Very well." Creighton paced back and forth in front of the witness stand. "You needed to consult with Mr. Malone on a business matter, so what did you do?"

"I went down the hall to the library."

Creighton looked at the jury as he addressed the next question to Summerlin. "And what did you see when you opened the door?"

"I saw Mr. Malone lying on the floor in front of the

desk. Mrs. Malone was kneeling beside him, a knife in her hand."

Even though everyone knew it was coming, the testimony caused a stir in the courtroom. Longarm crossed his arms over his chest. It was going to be hard for Janice to get around that damning bit of evidence.

"I'm sure you were quite shocked at this dreadful scene," Creighton said. "What did you do then, Mr. Summerlin?"

"Yes, I was shocked. More than that, I was fearful for my own life. I saw the expression on Mrs. Malone's face when she turned her head to look at me, and I was afraid she would come after me next. So I turned and ran back to my office."

"Why did you retreat there, Mr. Summerlin?"

"I keep a pistol in my desk. I wanted to get it so that I could defend myself if Mrs. Malone tried to stab me, too."

Janice was on her feet instantly. "Objection! It hasn't been proven that Mrs. Malone stabbed anyone."

"Sustained," Judge Walton growled. "The jury will disregard that part of the witness's answer."

Creighton nodded, unperturbed. "Leaving aside the question of whether or not Mrs. Malone stabbed her husband, you were still afraid that she might pose a threat to *your* life, is that correct, Mr. Summerlin?"

"Yes," Summerlin said firmly. "I didn't stop to think about whether or not anyone else could have been responsible for Mr. Malone's death. I just drew the obvious conclusion and took steps to protect myself from being the next victim."

"Objection!" Janice said. "The witness, in his own words, is drawing a conclusion."

"He is speaking to his own state of mind at the time, Your Honor," Creighton said.

Walton considered for a second, then said, "Overruled. Proceed, Mr. Creighton."

"What happened after you left the library? Did you return immediately to that room once you had procured your weapon?"

Summerlin shook his head. "No, I, ah, waited for several minutes in my office."

Cowered was probably more like it, thought Longarm.

"What transpired during that time?"

"I heard Mrs. Malone scream several times, and I heard the front door of the house open. Then, a few moments later, there were footsteps in the hallway. I decided that I should investigate, so I returned to the library."

"What did you find there?"

"I found that Mrs. Malone had left the house and then returned with a man who was unknown to me. Both of them were in the library with Mr. Malone's body. I discovered later that the man was a federal law enforcement officer Mrs. Malone encountered in the street outside."

Longarm frowned. Summerlin wasn't saying a word about trying to ventilate him. That would have made him look too panic-stricken and maybe not a thoroughly dependable witness.

"Then Miss Malone returned home from a social engagement and found that her father had been . . . found that her father was dead. She was quite upset, naturally. I tried to comfort her while Marshal Long—the man who had come in with Mrs. Malone—took charge of matters. He sent for the Denver police. They arrived and questioned everyone, and that's really the end of it as far as I was concerned."

"The State thanks you, Mr. Summerlin. Your testimony has been, I'm sure, a revelation to us all." Creighton returned to his table and sat down.

"Cross-examination, Miss Parmalee?" Walton asked as Janice was getting to her feet.

"Yes, Your Honor." Janice came out from behind her table and approached the witness. "Mr. Summerlin, you said that Mr. and Mrs. Malone fought frequently. Do you know what the subject of those arguments was?"

Summerlin stiffed. "I don't stick my nose into other people's private business."

Janice tilted her head slightly to one side. "You claim to have heard them shouting at each other, and yet you never overheard them well enough to know what they were arguing *about*?"

Summerlin fidgeted and looked at Creighton, but the prosecuting attorney kept his features carefully blank. He couldn't help Summerlin with this one, Longarm thought.

"Mrs. Malone was upset," Summerlin finally said.

"Upset about what?"

"She claimed that Mr. Malone . . . well, that Mr. Malone was being unfaithful to her."

"She claimed, in fact, that he was keeping a mistress. Isn't that true, Mr. Summerlin?"

Summerlin's head jerked in a nod. "That's what she said," he admitted.

"Was it true? Did Mr. Malone have a mistress?"

"Objection, Your Honor," Creighton said. "Mr. Malone is not on trial here, and his personal life is no business of this court!"

"Sustained," Walton ruled. "Move on, Miss Parmalee."

"Of course, Your Honor." Janice turned back to Summerlin. "You testified that you saw Mrs. Malone on her knees next to Mr. Malone's body, and that she had a knife in her hand."

"That's right," Summerlin said.

"Where was the knife?"

"I told you. In her hand."

Janice smiled thinly. "Where was the *blade* of the knife, Mr. Summerlin?"

Summerlin cleared his throat, thought about it, then said grudgingly, "In Mr. Malone's chest."

"In other words, you saw Mrs. Malone holding the *handle* of the knife that was buried in her husband's chest?"

Longarm saw Estelle's shoulders twitch a little.

"That's right."

"But you did *not* see her stab Mr. Malone?"

"Well . . . no. But why else would she have had hold of the knife?"

"Perhaps to pull it out after she found him there mortally wounded?"

Creighton came to his feet and said, "Objection, Your Honor! Now it is counsel for the defense who is speculating!"

"Sustained."

"I'll withdraw that, Your Honor," Janice said. "Mr. Summerlin, you said you feared for your life, that you thought the defendant might come after you next. Why is that?"

"Well, it seemed obvious to me what had happened, and I thought she might—"

"Prior to this, did Mrs. Malone ever threaten you?"

"No, not really. But she was always cold to me, as if she didn't like me." Summerlin glared. He must have known how weak that answer sounded.

"She didn't *like* you," Janice repeated. "To go from not liking someone to chasing them with a knife is quite a jump, isn't it, Mr. Summerlin?"

"Objection!" roared Creighton.

"Your Honor, I'm trying to establish that Mrs. Malone had no history of violence toward Mr. Malone or Mr. Summerlin or anyone else."

Walton's lips went in and out as he thought it over, then he said, "I'll overrule the objection. But tread lightly with your questioning, Miss Parmalee."

"Yes, Your Honor. Mr. Summerlin, did you ever see Mrs. Malone act in a violent manner toward her husband?"

"She shouted at him." Summerlin shrugged. "But that's all."

"In fact, you never observed her to act in a violent manner toward anyone, did you?"

"No," Summerlin said, his voice low. Longarm figured Janice would make him repeat it, but evidently she was satisfied, because she turned away from the witness stand.

"No further questions at this time, Your Honor."

Creighton was on his feet immediately. "Mr. Summerlin, during the arguments between Mr. and Mrs. Malone, did you ever hear Mrs. Malone *say* anything that could be construed as a threat?"

Summerlin looked and sounded more sure of himself now. "Yes, I did. Several times she told him he would be sorry for treating her the way he did. She told him she would *make* him sorry." He shot a triumphant glance at the defense table. Janice ignored him.

"Thank you, Mr. Summerlin."

"The witness may step down," Judge Walton said. He looked at Creighton.

The prosecuting attorney said, "The State calls Miss Natalie Malone."

Chapter 9

Creighton had started the ball with his strongest evidence, the discovery by Summerlin of Estelle Malone kneeling beside her husband's body, clutching the knife in her hand. By the time Natalie came home later, her father was already dead and the house was in an uproar. But Creighton used Natalie's testimony to establish that when she left the house earlier in the evening, things had been openly hostile between her father and her stepmother.

"Of course, that was nothing unusual," Natalie said. "They were always fighting. That woman made my poor father's life a living hell."

Longarm saw Janice grimace and knew she was probably thinking about objecting, but she remained in her chair at the defense table.

Natalie made a very appealing witness, thought Longarm. She still wore black, but she had lifted the veil on her hat so that her pale, lovely face was plainly visible. Her bottom lip trembled just so when she talked about seeing her father's body on the floor of the library, and her upper lip curled just the right amount when she referred to Estelle as "that woman." The gents in the jury box were very attentive as she gave her testimony.

"This is a difficult question for me to ask, Miss Malone," Creighton continued, "but do you believe there was any truth to the accusations your stepmother made against your father when they argued?"

"Are you talking about that ridiculous business of him having a . . . a *mistress*?" Natalie almost whispered the word. She shook her head. Tears shone in her eyes. "Never. My father was faithful to Estelle. He loved her, though I can't understand why."

Estelle Malone bowed her head and stared at the defense table, clearly shaken.

"So to the best of your knowledge," Creighton concluded, "on the evening of your father's death, there was no one else in the house with him except your stepmother, with whom he had been having a day-long argument over her false charges and vicious, baseless suspicions, and his close friend and loyal employee Howard Summerlin, who was closeted in his own small office hard at work?"

"That is correct," Natalie said.

"Thank you, Miss Malone. I have no further questions."

Janice rose to her feet. "Miss Malone. You have my sympathy on the loss of your father. As one who knows the . . . fear . . . of losing a parent, I am sure the reality is much, much worse."

Natalie looked surprised. "Thank you," she murmured.

"However," Janice continued, coming out from behind the table now, "I must ask you the same question that I asked Mr. Summerlin: Did you ever observe your stepmother behave in a violent manner toward your father?"

"She said terrible things to him, called him awful names."

"But she never attempted to injure him physically in any way?"

Natalie hesitated, then said, "No. Not while I was there."

Creighton, who had resumed his seat, stood up again. "Your Honor," he said, "the State will stipulate that Mrs. Malone has no history of physical violence against her late husband or anyone else. Otherwise I anticipate that

Miss Parmalee will be asking that same question of everyone in Denver who had the slightest acquaintance with the Malones." His droll tone brought a small wave of laughter from the spectators. Creighton smiled in acknowledgment, then grew serious as he went on, "However, the lack of such a history in no way precludes the possibility of Mrs. Malone resorting to violence in the heat of the moment as she argued with her husband."

Judge Walton looked at Janice and said, "You heard the prosecutor, Miss Parmalee. We all understand that Mrs. Malone didn't go around trying to stab people all the time."

"Certainly, Your Honor, but surely the court would not seek to try to limit a reasonable line of questioning—"

"Courts limit questioning all the time," Walton broke in. "And it's my job to decide what's reasonable. Now, let's get on with it, shall we?"

Janice took the rebuke gracefully and said, "Yes, Your Honor," but Longarm could see that her back was stiff with anger, some of it no doubt directed at herself. She had almost blundered badly. She turned back to Natalie and said, "You've testified, Miss Malone, that your father was alone with your stepmother that night . . ."

"That's right."

"With the exception of Mr. Summerlin."

Natalie frowned a little. "Well, yes. Howard was there."

"Did it ever occur to you that Mr. Summerlin might have attacked your father?"

That blunt question set the courtroom abuzz again, and from his seat in the spectators' section, Summerlin exclaimed, "What? That's outrageous!"

Judge Walton slammed his gavel on the bench and then pointed it at Summerlin. "Mr. Summerlin, be quiet! You've had your turn on the stand."

Creighton was on his feet again. "Your Honor, I object! No charge has been brought against Mr. Summerlin. He has been nothing but cooperative with the police and the office of the prosecuting attorney—"

"Which he certainly would be," Janice cut in, "if it was in his best interest that someone else be convicted of Jericho Malone's murder!"

Walton gaveled them both to silence. "That's enough! Your objection is overruled, Mr. Creighton. The witness will answer the question."

Janice looked at Natalie and asked, "Would you like me to repeat it?"

"No, that won't be necessary," Natalie replied icily. "And no, it never occurred to me that Mr. Summerlin might have attacked my father, because the very idea is ludicrous. Howard was devoted to my father. Besides, you've seen him. Honestly, does he look like a murderer to you?"

Summerlin, who had been looking indignant, now blinked and looked as if he wasn't sure if he had just been insulted or not. Longarm had to glance down at the floor to suppress the grin that spread across his face at Summerlin's discomfiture.

"Anyone can look like a murderer, Miss Malone," Janice said. "You don't deny, do you, that it's possible Mr. Summerlin stabbed your father instead of my client?"

"I don't believe it for a second . . . but I suppose it's possible."

Creighton said, "Your Honor, this character assassination on the part of defense counsel is shameful and scandalous! The police questioned Mr. Summerlin in the course of their investigation. Other than the fact that he was in the house, they found no reason whatsoever to believe that he might be a suspect in this crime. He has always been a faithful employee to Mr. Malone, and in his own words, a friend. And no one—no one!—has disputed that!"

Walton glowered at Creighton. "Is there an objection in there somewhere, Counsel, or were you just making a speech?"

"I'm through with this witness anyway," Janice said, turning to go back to the defense table.

"Redirect?" grated Walton.

Creighton shook his head. He was still glaring at Janice.

The judge told Natalie to step down. Creighton called the Malone gardener to the stand next. His name was Ed Carlson, and Creighton questioned him only briefly, establishing that Carlson and his wife, who served as cook and housekeeper, were in their own quarters on the night of Malone's murder. When asked to cross-examine, Janice stood up and said quietly, "No questions for this witness, Your Honor."

Alice Carlson was the next one to take the stand, confirming in her testimony what her husband had said. Once again, however, Creighton brought out the long-running argument between Jericho and Estelle Malone, since Mrs. Carlson had been in the Malone mansion all day with plenty of opportunities to overhear the heated clash. When questioned about the subject, Mrs. Carlson knotted her hands together in her lap and looked down at the floor. "I'm a servant, sir," she said. "I don't go mindin' the business of the folks I work for."

"Of course not, Mrs. Carlson," Creighton said smoothly and gently. "But you couldn't fail to hear what was going on that day, could you?"

She sniffed and said, "They was goin' at it so loud I don't see how the whole blessed city didn't hear 'em."

"It was the usual argument?"

"Oh, yes. The missus, she was goin' on about how the mister had himself a ladyfriend, and the mister was denyin' it. It didn't do no good, though. It never did."

"Thank you, Mrs. Carlson. That's all."

Janice stood up and said, "Mrs. Carlson, how did you feel about your employers?"

"Employer," Mrs. Carlson corrected stiffly. "I worked for Mr. Malone."

"And you were quite fond of him, weren't you?"

"He was a good man."

"I'm sure he was. But you didn't like Mrs. Malone, did you?"

Again the sniff. "I didn't have no complaints."

"But she had complaints about you and your slipshod work, didn't she?"

"Slipshod! Well, I never! The missus was just impossible to please, that's all."

"So you *didn't* like her, just as I said."

"The feelin' was mutual." Mrs. Carlson stared slit-eyed at Estelle.

"No more questions for this witness, Your Honor."

"Step down, madam." Judge Walton leaned back in his chair, reached inside his robes, and brought out a watch. Looking at it, he said, "Who's your next witness, Mr. Creighton?"

"The State will call Deputy United States Marshal Custis Long, Your Honor."

Longarm straightened from his position where he'd been lounging against the wall in the back of the courtroom.

"Not today, you won't. It's too late in the afternoon," Walton declared. He snapped his watch closed and put it away. "Court stands adjourned until nine o'clock tomorrow morning." He picked up the gavel and smacked it against the bench.

The hubbub in the courtroom started soft and then gradually rose as Walton disappeared into his chambers. Still holding his hat in his hand, Longarm went forward and stepped through the railing to join Creighton behind the defense table. The prosecuting attorney was putting away his papers and talking to his associate. He glanced over at Longarm and said, "Oh, there you are, Marshal. I'm sorry we didn't get to you today. I'm sure you're anxious to get back to your duties."

"Naw, Billy Vail said I could have until the end of the trial."

"I don't know that that will be necessary. We'll get your testimony out of the way first thing tomorrow, and then you can go about your business. Subject to being recalled, of course."

Longarm figured he had clashed one too many times with Creighton. The prosecutor didn't want him hanging around anymore. Longarm wasn't so sure he was going to be gotten rid of that easily, though.

He didn't argue the point, just nodded instead. Turning, he looked toward the defense table and saw Janice talking earnestly to Estelle Malone. Estelle looked worried, but Janice appeared to be trying to reassure her. The guards were waiting to take Estelle back to her cell. Janice put a hand on her arm and squeezed for a moment, then nodded. The guards moved in and ushered Estelle out of the courtroom through the side door.

"Miss Parmalee acquitted herself rather well for a beginner, don't you think?" Creighton asked from behind Longarm.

"She did all right," he replied.

"Pity she's going to lose this case. Your testimony will be all the jury needs to hear to confirm what they must already be thinking."

Longarm turned toward Creighton again. "How do you figure that? I didn't see Mrs. Malone in nearly as incriminating a position as Summerlin did."

"Oh, come now. You saw the woman come running into the street with blood all over her nightclothes. She was hysterical."

"That don't mean she's a killer."

"There was no blood on Summerlin, was there? He was the only other person with the opportunity to commit the crime."

"That we know of," Longarm said slowly.

Creighton glared at him. "What the deuce do you mean by *that*?"

"We know that Mrs. Malone and Summerlin were alone in the house with Malone when the evening started," said Longarm. "How do we know somebody else didn't get in there, stab Malone, and then light a shuck out?"

"Light a shuck? I'm not sure—"

"Leave. In a hurry." Longarm slid a cheroot from his

vest pocket and put it unlit in his mouth. "Could've happened that way."

He left Creighton standing there, frowning, and as he went out of the courtroom, Longarm turned over the new theory in his mind. Crime was usually simple, and it was a mistake to try to complicate it too much. The easiest answer was nearly always the right one.

But someone else *could* have been at the Malone mansion that night, he realized. Dan Hubbard and the other police would have checked on that, but they were convinced they already had their murderer. They might have missed something.

The question was, who else would have had a reason to want Jericho Malone dead?

Longarm couldn't answer that one, not without doing some poking around of his own. Billy Vail wasn't expecting him back at the office until the trial was over . . .

On the courthouse steps, Longarm snapped a lucifer into life and held the flame to the end of his cheroot. He had just taken a puff when Janice Parmalee said from behind him, "Marshal Long?"

Chapter 10

Longarm turned around and saw her looking up at him. He tugged on the brim of his hat and said, "Miss Parmalee."

"I was wondering if I could talk to you, Marshal."

"I ain't so sure that's a good idea," Longarm said, his eyes narrowing. "We're on opposite sides in this court case, you know. I ain't ever been one to worry overmuch about decorum, but there's some things that just don't look right."

"Of course. I was just wondering if . . . I mean, you were so helpful when my father was . . . was stricken . . . I'd like to repay your kindness by taking you to dinner."

Longarm frowned. "You want to take *me* out?"

"Yes," Janice said, her voice firmer now. "And I know, it's not proper for a lady to ask a gentlemen to dine with her. But I've been doing things most of my life that aren't considered proper behavior for a lady." She paused, then blushed hotly, no doubt because she had realized how her last comment might have sounded to Longarm. "Being an attorney, I mean," she added quickly.

"Sure, I knew that," Longarm said. "Just dinner? No talkin' about the court case?"

"Just dinner," Janice promised.

"Well, I don't see anything wrong with that. And if anybody does—meanin' Abercrombie Creighton—that's his problem, not mine."

"Thank you. I'm afraid I'll have to prevail upon you to select the restaurant. I don't know that much about Denver . . ."

Longarm took her arm. "I'll find us a nice place," he said.

"I have to see about my father first, but if you'll tell me where to meet you . . ."

"I'll go to the hospital with you," Longarm offered. Just in case more bad news was waiting for Janice, he didn't want her to be alone when she received it.

He hailed a cab. As the horse pulled the carriage through the streets with a brisk clip-clop of hooves, Longarm sat next to Janice and was aware of the warmth of her hip next to his. She kept her eyes downcast and didn't look at him. He had a feeling she'd never had much to do with men, probably having devoted herself to her father and her own legal career. He was drawn to her anyway, which was unusual. Most of the time, he was attracted to a lustier, earthier sort of woman. He had deflowered a few virgins in his life, but it had been quite a while. Of course, he didn't know for sure that Janice Parmalee *was* a virgin, and it was a hell of a leap from dinner to deflowering, but shoot, these were just idle thoughts anyway, he told himself.

A white-capped nurse at the hospital told them that there was no change in Herbert Parmalee's condition. He was stable and seemed to be resting comfortably, but he still hadn't regained consciousness. Janice asked that she be notified immediately if there were any new developments. Longarm contributed the name of the restaurant where he planned to take her, then Janice added the name of the hotel where she and her father were staying.

"I'll come by again in the morning before court resumes," Janice told the nurse, who promised to pass along the information to Herbert Parmalee's doctor.

Janice sighed as they left the hospital. "It's so hard to concentrate on anything else," she said. "All I can do is worry about Father."

"Looked to me like you were concentrating just fine in court," Longarm told her.

"Yes, but that helped keep me distracted. Besides, I owe Mrs. Malone my best effort. And I thought we weren't supposed to discuss the case."

"We ain't discussin' it," Longarm said. He whistled for a cab.

He took her to one of the best steakhouses in Denver, after Janice assured him that money was no object. "Father's practice has been quite successful," she said.

The place was busy, the clientele about evenly split between townspeople and cattlemen who were in Denver on business. Janice looked wide-eyed at all the boots and broad-brimmed hats in evidence.

"Denver seems so cosmopolitan," she said as she and Longarm sipped the wine that the waiter had brought them, "but it really is right on the edge of the Wild West, isn't it?"

"You don't have to dig very deep under the surface to scratch the frontier," Longarm said.

"Are there ever any Indian attacks?"

Longarm tried not to smile. "Not in these parts. There are plenty of places west of the Mississippi, though, where your hair might not be too safe."

"I imagine in your job you deal with notorious outlaws all the time."

"Some," Longarm said with a shrug. "I reckon desperadoes will always be with us in one form or another. Just look at Washington."

She stared at him for a second, then laughed. "At least you aimed your gibe at the politicians, instead of lawyers."

"I've known plenty of honest hombres who practiced law. You must, too."

"Of course. Otherwise I never would have gone into it myself."

"That must've been hard. I don't reckon there were too many other gals at law school with you."

"None, in fact," Janice said. "But I didn't let that deter me. Father always says that I was quite willful and stubborn as a child and always had to get what I wanted. I'm afraid I haven't changed much as an adult."

"A fella's got to set his sights on something and stick to it," Longarm said. "Reckon it's the same for a gal."

Plates full of steak and potatoes and rolls arrived, along with side dishes of vegetables and fruit. Janice looked at the spread and said, "Oh, my. I'm not sure I can eat all of this."

"Just eat what you want," Longarm told her. "You're payin' for it."

She laughed and dug in, and for a delicate little thing, she had a surprisingly hearty appetite, Longarm saw over the next half hour. He could tell she was still worried about her father, naturally enough, but she tried to keep the dinner conversation light and lively, drawing Longarm out by asking him to tell her about his career as a lawman for Uncle Sam. He obliged by spinning some of the more colorful yarns about his life, leaving out the gamier parts.

"If you want to go back farther than that," he concluded, "I grew up in West-by-God Virginia but came out here after the Late Unpleasantness."

"You mean the War Between the States?"

"Yes, ma'am."

"Did you fight in it?"

"I wasn't much more'n a younker at the time, but yes, I took up arms. Don't ask me on which side, though, because I tend to disremember."

"What did you do before you became a deputy marshal?"

"Cowboyed, mostly," Longarm said. "Helped bring some herds of longhorns up the trail from Texas to the railhead." He touched his luxuriant mustache. "That's when I grew this. It's called a longhorn, too."

"It's very becoming," Janice said, then blushed again. She was just about the blushingest gal Longarm had ever seen.

When they were finished with their meal, Janice declined the offer of brandy. "I need to get back to the hotel and start going over my notes for court tomorrow."

Longarm grinned. "Figuring out how to cross-examine me, eh?" He held up his hands, palms out. "Sorry. Didn't mean to bring that up."

"That's all right, Marshal. I know that when the time comes, you and I will both do what we need to do."

"Yes, ma'am," Longarm said.

He escorted her to her hotel and left her in the lobby. It was a mite early to turn in, but he couldn't work up any enthusiasm for paying a visit to any of the saloons or gambling halls he frequented, so he headed back to his rented room.

When he reached the boardinghouse, the landlady was sitting in the parlor, working on her knitting. She glanced in Longarm's direction as he came through the foyer. He tipped his hat to her, but with a frown, she sniffed in disapproval and looked down at her knitting. Longarm wondered what the hell that was about. The landlady was acting almost like he had a woman in his room.

He glanced up the stairs. Maybe there *was* a woman in his room. Only one way to find out, he told himself.

When he reached the top of the stairs, he slipped the derringer out of his vest pocket and held it in his hand as he approached the door of his room. He had reloaded the barrel he'd discharged in the courtroom that morning, so once again he had two .41-caliber cartridges at his disposal in case of trouble. With his other hand, he took out his key.

Longarm rattled the key in the lock as he was turning it, then stepped quickly to one side. Nobody fired a scattergun through the door, so he reached over, twisted the knob, and shoved the door open. Light spilled through the doorway, telling Longarm that someone had lit the lamp in the room.

"Really, Marshal," said a woman's voice, "you don't have to be so cautious. I'm not waiting to ambush you."

Longarm recognized the voice as Natalie Malone's. He stepped into the doorway and on into the room, but he didn't put the derringer away just yet. He wanted to make sure Natalie was alone first.

She was. She stood near the window, wearing the same mourning outfit she had worn in court that day. The veil on the hat was still up, as it had been when she testified. She smiled at Longarm and asked, "Are you always this careful, Marshal Long?"

Longarm grunted. "I'm still alive, ain't I?" He slipped the derringer into his vest pocket, then said, "Pardon me for bein' blunt, Miss Malone, but what are you doin' here?"

"I want to talk to you about the trial."

"I ain't sure that's a good idea," Longarm said.

"Why not? You didn't seem to be too worried about the legal proprieties when you were helping Miss Parmalee in the courtroom . . . or when you were having dinner with her this evening."

Longarm frowned. "How'd you know about that?"

"Howard told me. He's been keeping an eye on you, Marshal. We're beginning to think that perhaps you won't be as good a witness for the prosecution as you should be, that perhaps you've been swayed by Miss Parmalee's dubious charms. Though I don't see why any man would be."

Longarm felt his temper rising. "I'll tell the truth when I'm on the witness stand," he said stiffly. "That's all I'll swear to do."

Natalie came a step closer to him. "But you saw it all for yourself, Marshal. You saw my stepmother with my father's blood on her clothes. Isn't that enough to convince you that she killed him?"

"It's enough to convince me she got his blood on her,"

Longarm said. "That don't say *how* it got there."

"But you're a lawman. You know how it looks—"

"All the evidence points to your stepmother," Longarm broke in. "Whether or not that's enough to convict her is up to the jury."

"You could go a long way toward convincing them if you testify that you think Estelle killed my father."

"I think she *could* have," Longarm said. "But that's all I can honestly testify to."

"But if Mr. Creighton asks you for your best opinion as a law enforcement officer—"

"Then Miss Parmalee will probably object that I'm drawing a conclusion."

"The judge will overrule her."

Longarm thought about how Judge Walton had run the trial so far and shrugged. "Maybe, maybe not. I'd hate to bet money on it either way."

Natalie began to pace back and forth. "You're just being stubborn," she said, allowing irritation to creep into her voice. "You know as well as I do that Estelle killed my father, you know that if you say that in court the jury will convict her, and yet you play these little games."

"I'm not playing any sort of game," Longarm said. "I don't much like what you're saying, neither. I reckon it's time for you to go, Miss Malone."

She stopped her pacing and stared at him. "You're kicking me out?"

"That's about the size of it," drawled Longarm.

She came closer to him, her eyes blazing with the emotions inside her. "What can I do, Marshal?" she asked. "What can I do to change your mind?" Suddenly, she was in his arms, her body pressed hotly to his. "How about this?"

And her mouth found his, kissing him hungrily.

Chapter 11

Longarm was human, right enough. He'd never denied that. And he wouldn't deny that Natalie Malone felt damned good wrapped in his arms like that, her body molded to his, her lips open and her tongue wetly seeking his. He enjoyed the sweet-tasting heat of her mouth and the softness of her breasts as they pressed against him. Her hips moved back and forth, expertly grinding her belly against his groin. His manhood began to rise, hardening into a long, thick shaft of flesh that prodded against her.

Natalie drew her head back slightly and smiled at him. "You see, Marshal," she said throatily, "I can make it worth your while to go along with what I want. I'm not as innocent as I look. I know all sorts of tricks that men like."

Longarm lifted a hand and let his fingertips play along the line of her jaw, then slid it around to the back of her neck. He held her head as he kissed her again, and this time she responded with even more passion. She reached between their bodies and caressed his stiff organ through his trousers. After a moment, she began fumbling with the buttons, obviously intending to free his manhood from the confines of trousers and underwear and take it in her hand.

Longarm didn't let her get that far. He broke the kiss this time, and as she smiled smugly at him, he said, "You know, for a rich gal, you sure are a cheap little whore, Miss Malone."

For a second, the harshness of his words didn't penetrate her brain. Then her eyes widened and she gasped in shock. "Wh-what did you say?"

Longarm's left arm was around her waist, his right hand still at the back of her neck. He kept his grip on her as he told her, "I said you were a cheap little whore. You reckon you can come in here, play a little slap-and-tickle with me, and get me to do whatever you damned well want, even if it means sayin' I think your stepmother killed your father and General George Armstrong Custer and the whole damned Seventh Cavalry!"

"What . . . How dare you . . . Why, I never—"

"Oh, I reckon you have," Longarm said dryly. "Probably a whole heap of times, with a bunch of different fellas. I don't hold a healthy appetite for rompin' against a gal, but I don't like it when she tries to buy me off with what's betwixt her legs." He was being deliberately crude now, which went against his natural penchant for chivalry, but Natalie had made him pure-dee mad.

She shoved against his chest. "Let go of me, you bastard!"

"Nope. Maybe I'll take what you were just offerin' me anyway, then testify however I want."

Now she was starting to look frightened. "You . . . you can't! That would be rape!"

"You were plenty willin' a minute ago."

"I'll scream—"

Longarm couldn't keep up the act any longer. He let go of her and stepped back, putting some distance between them. "Don't worry," he said, his mouth twisting like he'd just bit into a sour apple. "What's left of your virtue is safe with me, Miss Malone."

"Oh!" Her face was flaming red with embarrassment and anger. Her hand came up and flashed toward his face.

Without even seeming to hurry, he caught her wrist before she could slap him. They stood there, frozen like that for a long moment, before Longarm said quietly, "I wouldn't push my luck if I was you, ma'am."

When he let go of her this time, she was the one who stepped back, stumbling a bit. She put a hand on the small table beside his bed to steady herself, then said, "I don't suppose it would do any good to start crying now, would it?"

"Not a damned bit."

Natalie sighed, shook her head, and said, "Shit. I just wanted—"

"I know what you wanted," Longarm said.

"No, you don't." She glared at him. "Yes, I was willing to play a little slap-and-tickle, as you so colorfully put it, with you if you'd agree to push my stepmother's guilt when you testify tomorrow. That would be a small price to pay to insure that witch winds up where she belongs, which is behind bars for the rest of her life, if not on the gallows."

"A small price," mused Longarm. "Thank you most to death for the compliment."

Natalie waved a hand. "You know what I mean."

"Yep, I reckon I do. You hate your stepmother, and you'll do anything to see that she's convicted."

"That's right. But it's only because she's *guilty*."

"The jury usually decides that," Longarm pointed out.

"They have to decide if she's guilty of murdering my father," Natalie said. "I *know* she's guilty of making him desperately unhappy, because I saw that with my own eyes."

The anguish creeping into her voice told Longarm that she was finally being sincere. He said, "I don't know about how the two of them got along, because I wasn't there. But just because she did one thing don't mean she did the other."

"But she had to! No one else was there."

"Howard Summerlin was."

Natalie shook her head. "I meant what I said in court. Howard would never have hurt Father. He's too big a toady for that."

"I wouldn't let him hear you say that, if I was you," cautioned Longarm. "He seems to be mighty fond of *you,* too. I reckon he's thinking you might feel grateful to him for all he's done to help out."

"I am grateful to—" Natalie stopped short, then went on in horror, "Wait a minute. You don't mean . . . You can't mean . . . that Howard thinks he and I . . . that we might ever . . ."

"I got a feeling you're about to either laugh or cry," said Longarm.

Her chin came up. "I won't do either one. But what you're suggesting is ludicrous. I'm grateful to Howard for everything he's done, but that's all. There could never be anything else between us."

"Doesn't matter whether you think so or not. He can still feel that way." Longarm scraped a thumbnail along the line of his jaw as he thought. "Maybe he even had the idea that if something happened to your father, you'd have to turn to him for help."

Natalie lifted a hand to her mouth. "Oh, my God. That's impossible. Howard would never . . . He wouldn't have the nerve . . ."

Longarm took out a cheroot and turned it over in his fingers. "Some fellas do mighty unexpected things where a woman's concerned."

"Still, I don't believe it."

"I ain't sayin' I do, either. It's just a possibility. Seems like nobody in this case is even considering any of those except the one that says your stepmother is guilty. That sort of bothers me."

"Is that why you're helping that Parmalee woman?"

"I ain't helpin' Miss Parmalee," Longarm said. "I went to the hospital with her when she went to check on her father, and then we had dinner together. But we agreed not to talk about the trial."

"I'm sure you stuck to that vow," Natalie said skeptically.

"As a matter of fact, we pretty much did. I was the one who almost strayed, and Miss Parmalee put me back on the straight and narrow."

Natalie looked at him for a second, then said, "I suppose I believe you. There's really nothing else I can do, is there?" She laughed hollowly. "Besides, it's almost as ludicrous to think that Miss Parmalee could tempt you as it is to believe that there could ever be anything between me and Howard Summerlin."

Longarm didn't understand why Natalie thought it was so far-fetched that he could be interested in Janice, but he didn't want to get into that argument right now. Instead, he said, "I give you my word, Miss Malone, that I'll testify as honestly as I can tomorrow, and let the chips fall where they may."

"I can't ask for any more than that." Natalie made a face. "Well, I can ask, but obviously I'm not going to get it." She started for the door, then paused as she reached it. Looking back over her shoulder at Longarm, she said, "Tell me the truth, though, Marshal . . . for a moment, you *were* tempted, weren't you?"

Longarm thought about it, then nodded. "I reckon I was."

He hadn't sworn any oath to tell the truth *now*.

The evening passed quietly after Natalie Malone left. Longarm spent it smoking and sipping from a bottle of Maryland rye while he thought about the case. He had no official connection to it, of course. He could give his testimony the next day as honestly as he could, then walk away from the whole thing with no stain on his conscience.

But the lawman in him was bothered by what he had seen so far during the trial. Estelle Malone wasn't being railroaded—there was plenty of evidence against her to justify an indictment and trial—but it seemed to Longarm that more attention should have been paid to the other possibilities. Nobody got to be as successful as Jericho Malone had been without making some enemies along the way. Maybe Estelle was on the verge of paying for the revenge that had been carried out by someone else.

Longarm pondered the situation long into the night before finally dozing off.

When he arrived at the courthouse the next morning, fresh from a breakfast of flapjacks, bacon, biscuits, gravy, and coffee, Longarm found Abercrombie Creighton waiting for him with a thunderous frown on his face. Without any greeting, Creighton demanded, "What's all this I hear about you having dinner with opposing counsel last night?"

"She's your opposing counsel, not mine," Longarm said. "Far as I'm concerned, Miss Parmalee is just a nice young lady who's worried because her daddy is sick."

"So you took it upon yourself to *comfort* the young woman," Creighton said with a sneer. "Your gallantry has outdone itself this time, Marshal."

Longarm sucked an eyetooth for a second, then said, "What's the penalty in this state for bustin' a loudmouthed lawyer in the mush?"

Creighton drew in a sharp breath and took a step back. "Are you threatening me?"

"Just askin' a legal question. As for Miss Parmalee, we didn't discuss the case or the trial. You can take my word for that, or you can go to hell." Longarm paused, then added, "Interestin', though, that Natalie Malone's been talking to you this morning."

"Of course Miss Malone has spoken to me," Creighton said stiffly. "She's a witness for the prosecution, not to mention one of the injured parties in this case."

"She tell you she came to see me last night?"

Creighton blinked and frowned. "No. What do you mean?"

"Ask her," Longarm suggested. Natalie could tell Creighton as much or as little as she wanted to about her visit to Longarm's room. He didn't really care anymore.

Longarm went past Creighton into the courtroom and found a seat. He wasn't going to stand up today. He cocked his right ankle on his left knee and balanced his hat on his leg. He was ready for whatever the morning brought.

Once again, the courtroom filled up quickly. When Janice Parmalee came in, she looked at Longarm, and he thought for a second she was going to smile at him before she caught herself. She wore a solemn expression as Estelle Malone was brought in and seated at the witness table.

Longarm wondered how Janice's father was doing this morning. He didn't have to wait long to find out. As soon as Judge Walton had come in and called the court to order, the judge asked, "Miss Parmalee, I trust your father is recovering from his collapse yesterday?"

Janice came to her feet. "As well as can be expected, Your Honor. He still has not regained consciousness."

"He has the court's prayers," Walton murmured. Then he rapped the gavel and was all business again as he said, "Mr. Creighton, call your next witness."

Creighton rose to his feet. "The State calls Marshal Custis Long."

Longarm was sworn in, gave his name and occupation, and then Creighton said, "Please tell us in your own words, Marshal, what happened to you and what you observed on the evening of Jericho Malone's death."

Longarm did so, sticking strictly to the facts as he remembered them, and he trusted his memory to be pretty good. Creighton didn't interrupt. He knew that some, if not all, of the jury members would have heard of Longarm and would be impressed with such clear testimony coming from a respected lawman.

When Longarm was finished, Creighton said, "Thank you, Marshal." He started to turn away as if he were finished, then he stopped and turned back toward the witness stand. Janice had been about to get up, but she settled down in her chair as Creighton once more approached the witness stand.

"Just one more thing. In your capacity as a lawman, have you investigated many murders?"

Longarm frowned. "Murder's a state crime, not a federal one. I work for the U.S. Justice Department."

"I understand that, Marshal," Creighton said, "but surely in your years of carrying a badge, you have encountered cases in which some innocent lost his or her life at the hands of a killer."

"Well, sure," Longarm said. He knew where Creighton was headed with this, and he had hoped to avoid it.

"So even though technically dealing with murder is not within your scope of duties as a federal marshal, you *do* have a considerable amount of practical experience with violent death?"

"I've seen more'n my share," Longarm replied, his voice hard.

"I would ask you, then, Marshal, in your professional opinion as a seasoned lawman with many years of experience, given the circumstances of Jericho Malone's death which you yourself have described for us, who do you consider the most likely person to have committed this crime?"

Longarm glanced at Janice Parmalee, but her face was carefully expressionless. Estelle was looking down at the table, as she did most of the time during the trial.

"Marshal?" Creighton prodded. "Would you like me to repeat the question?"

"Not hardly," Longarm said. "I reckon under the circumstances, the most likely person to have killed Malone was his wife. But that don't mean—"

"You've answered the question, Marshal. Thank you."

Janice stood up as Creighton went back to the prosecution table. She stayed where she was instead of approaching the witness stand. "You were about to say something else, Marshal," she began.

"Objection," Creighton said. "Not responsive to the question."

"Not to *your* question, perhaps," Janice said.

"Overruled," Walton said. "Miss Parmalee has a right to cross-examine the witness, Mr. Creighton."

"Of course, Your Honor."

Janice looked at Longarm and asked, "What were you about to say, Marshal Long?"

"Just that because I said Mrs. Malone is probably the most likely to have killed her husband, that don't mean she actually did."

"You mean you think Mrs. Malone *didn't* kill her husband?" Janice asked quickly.

"I didn't say that, either," Longarm replied. "I don't know who killed Malone. I didn't see it happen."

"Thank you, Marshal Long. No further questions."

Creighton popped back up. "Do you believe Mrs. Malone killed her husband, Marshal?"

"I don't know—"

"I didn't ask what you know, Marshal, I asked you what you believe!"

"Objection! He's calling for a conclusion on the part of the witness!"

"I am calling for an opinion, a matter of belief!"

"A witness can only testify on matters of fact!"

"It's a *fact* that a man can have an opinion, isn't it?"

Janice and Creighton were shouting at each other now. Judge Walton hammered with his gavel. "Both of you shut up!" he bellowed. "The objection is sustained. A man's entitled to have an opinion."

Creighton said, "The witness should be forced to answer the question, Your Honor."

"Now he's treating Marshal Long as a hostile witness, Your Honor!"

"Well, maybe he is!" Creighton shot back.

"Now hold on!" Longarm said from the witness stand, forestalling another round of gavel-pounding from Judge Walton. "I ain't never been hostile to the law since I pinned on a badge. I already said I don't know who killed Malone, and *that's* my opinion! Mrs. Malone could have, but so could that fella Summerlin or somebody else entirely."

From where he and Natalie were sitting in the spectators' seats, Howard Summerlin bounded up and said, "Your Honor, how often do I have to be falsely accused during this trial? This is completely outrageous—"

"Sit down!" Walton barked at Summerlin.

"Your Honor," Creighton said, "I again request that the witness be compelled to answer—"

"He answered you already, Counselor. He said his opinion is he doesn't know. Do you have any more questions?"

Creighton ground his teeth together for a second, then said, "No, Your Honor."

"Miss Parmalee?"

"No further questions, Your Honor," Janice said.

"Then the witness is excused! Marshal Long, step down."

"I'll be glad to, Your Honor," Longarm said. He stood up, stalked across to the railing, slapped the gate aside, plucked up his hat from the chair where he had been sitting earlier, clapped it on his head, and walked out of the courtroom without looking back.

He had seldom in his life been so glad to get the hell out of a place.

Chapter 12

Longarm didn't know what happened during the trail the rest of the day. He spent the time in the Crystal Palace instead of the courthouse, playing five card stud, smoking cheroots, and nursing a bottle of Tom Moore. The sanctum of the back room at the gambling hall and saloon was just what he needed.

By evening he was up nearly forty dollars in the game and the tension brought on by his court appearance that morning had vanished. His stomach was growling with hunger, too. He looked around at the other card players and said, "Reckon I'll cash in, boys."

"You sure, Custis?" asked one of them, a cattleman named Blake. "You've got some of my money there."

"Won it fair and square, too," Longarm said with a grin. "You'll have to wait until next time to try to get it back."

"Well, all right, if you're sure," Blake said with a good-natured smile of his own.

Longarm stood up, scooped the pile of bills and coins in front of him into his hat, and went to the back room's small bar to sort it out and stow it away. One of the saloon's barmaids was working there, a woman about thirty with long blond hair. She wore a red gown that left the upper third of her fine breasts exposed.

"Looks like you won, Marshal," she said as Longarm put his hat on the bar.
"A little. The stakes were pretty small."
"You're cashing in?"
"That's right."
"Care for another drink before you go?"
Longarm thought about it, then nodded. "Brandy, this time. I've had enough rye to last me for a while."
The blonde put a crystal snifter on the bar and poured liquor into it from a short, fat bottle. "What are your plans for the evening?" she asked.
"Thought I'd get some supper, then make an early night of it."
She leaned forward a little, so that more of the valley between her breasts was exposed. "Care for some company?"
Longarm took a sip of the fiery brandy and relished the warmth that came from it and filled his body. He was experiencing another sort of warmth, too, as the blonde looked at him with an unmistakable message in her blue eyes.
"That sounds mighty fine," he said. "Might be just what I've been needin'."

"Just lie back," she said as she pressed her hands lightly against his shoulders. "Let me do the work for a while."
Longarm reclined on the pillows she had piled up behind him. After dinner, they had come back here to her place, rather than going to his room. It was a fairly nice room, definitely a step or two up from a whore's crib. The blonde, whose name was Candace, wasn't a soiled dove, either, at least not all the time. Tonight, for instance, she had made it clear that she was doing this because she'd seen Longarm around the Crystal Palace and admired him.
Candace was pretty admirable, too, as Longarm had seen when she peeled out of her duds and stood nude before him, her blond hair loose now and flowing around her shoulders. Her breasts were full and firm and rounded,

her belly almost flat, flowing into womanly hips and strong thighs. The triangle of fine-spun hair at the juncture of her thighs was a shade darker than that on her head. She had let Longarm take a good long look at her, then undressed him and told him to lie down.

He was already fully erect, his shaft jutting up strongly from his groin. Candace began massaging his thighs, digging her strong, capable fingers into his muscles. She moved his legs apart so that she could knead his inner thighs. From time to time she reached up and cupped the heavy sac that hung just below his hard manhood.

She moved her hands to his abdomen, still massaging, and occasionally she brushed the back of a hand or a forearm against his shaft. The touches were tantalizing, and Longarm's fleshy pole throbbed with the desire that was building up inside him.

Finally she took his organ in both hands, wrapping her warm fingers around it and sliding her palms up and down. "You're a double handful, Custis," she said with a smile, "just like I thought you'd be."

Her stroking motions milked a large, pearlescent drop of fluid from the slit in the middle of the head. Candace leaned closer, and her mouth opened. Her tongue came out and lapped up the fluid. Longarm's shaft jumped in anticipation of more delights.

He didn't have long to wait. Candace nuzzled kisses up and down the length of the pole, then moved her mouth to his balls and drew them gently in, one after the other. Her fingertip raked maddeningly across the sensitive area just below the sac.

Finally, she lifted her head and moved her lips back to the tip of his shaft. She spread her mouth open wide and lowered it over the head, engulfing him in sweet warmth. His pole was so thick she could take only a few inches of it into her mouth, but that was enough. She started sucking insistently.

Longarm closed his eyes and gave himself over to the sensations she was arousing inside him. This was pure pleasure, simple and unadorned, so much so that within too short a time, he felt his climax approaching. He opened his eyes and raised his head a little so that he could look down at Candace. "Better hold off there," he warned her.

She lifted her head and tossed her blond hair back. "I want you to let it go in my mouth," she said. "And watch me while you're filling me up."

"You're sure?"

"Please, Custis."

Anything to oblige a lady, that was his motto. He propped himself up on his elbows so he would have a good view as she went back to sucking him. He saw his shaft disappearing into her mouth. She took in more and more of it, until it seemed certain that she would choke. Somehow, though, she didn't.

She fondled his balls again, and that was enough to shove Longarm over the edge. He shuddered and his hips came up off the bed as his climax erupted. With each spurt of his thick seed, he gave a little jabbing thrust into Candace's mouth. It seemed that he was emptying himself right down to the core of his being. He spent so much that Candace's mouth couldn't contain it all, and she couldn't swallow fast enough. The fluid welled past her lips and flowed down over her chin and throat.

Finally, with one last jerk of his hips, Longarm was finished. He was sated, and lassitude filled his body, causing all his muscles to relax and send him sagging back onto the bed. His broad chest, matted with brown hair, rose and fell rapidly as he tried to catch his breath.

Candace lifted her head from his drenched, softening organ. She used her hand to squeeze out the last drop of his fluid and licked it up. She laughed softly and smiled up at Longarm.

"I must look a mess," she said.

"You look mighty pretty to me," Longarm told her truthfully.

She swung her legs off the bed and said, "I'll be back in a minute."

She stood up and went behind a screen in the corner of the room. Longarm figured there was a dressing table and a basin of water back there. Sure enough, when Candace came back to the bed a moment later, her face was clean and she had a wet cloth in her hand. She used it to wash Longarm's shaft and the area around it before the spilled seed could turn even stickier.

"That was nice as nice can be," Longarm told her. "Reckon you wound up doing all the work, though."

"Oh, no," Candace said. "We're not through yet, Custis." She stretched out on the bed, raised her arms over her head so that her fine breasts rose beautifully, and pulled her knees up. Her thighs parted as she spread her legs. The pink folds of feminine flesh thus revealed were already wet and shining with anticipation. "It's my turn now."

Longarm grinned and bent to his task. It was no chore at all.

"And when you're finished," Candace said as she reached down and began to caress his shoulders, "you'll be ready to do it the usual way."

That sounded like a mighty fine plan to Longarm.

What with one thing and another—and Candace proved to be mighty inventive when it came to those other things—it was late in the evening when Longarm got back to the boardinghouse.

Though he had been successful for most of the day in putting the trial of Estelle Malone and everything connected with it out of his mind, he found those thoughts sneaking back into his brain as he walked through the darkened streets. He wondered if Abercrombie Creighton had rested the State's case yet, and if Janice Parmalee had begun the defense. He was curious, too, about the health of Herbert Parmalee. He even thought about going by the hospital to see about the lawyer but decided against it. Maybe in the morning.

He opened the gate in the picket fence that surrounded the small yard in front of the boardinghouse. The house itself was dark. All the other boarders likely had gone to bed.

As Longarm started up the walk toward the porch, a figure moved out of the shadows. His instinctive, habitual caution took over and made his hand start toward the Colt holstered in the cross-draw rig. Before he could draw the gun, though, a woman's voice said urgently, "Wait, Marshal, it's all right!" Longarm recognized the shape, too, as belonging to a woman. She wore a gown with a bustle and a broad-brimmed hat.

He didn't know the voice, but clearly she knew who he was. He relaxed, but only slightly. His hand was still ready to wrap itself around the butt of the Colt at less than a second's notice.

"Evenin', ma'am," he said. "What can I do for you?"

"I hope I can do something for you, Marshal," the woman said.

He relaxed a little more. "Sorry, I just came from there," he said. "Maybe some other time . . ."

The woman laughed. "You flatter me. I know what a handsome man you are, Marshal Long. But I'm afraid you've misunderstood me. What you think isn't the reason I came here tonight at all."

"Suppose you tell me why you're here, then," Longarm suggested.

"Of course. My name is Belle Cardwell, though I doubt that means anything to you."

"No, ma'am, I'm afraid not."

"You've heard a great deal about me lately, however, whether you realize it or not." The woman came a step closer to Longarm. "You see, Marshal Long, I was Jericho Malone's mistress."

Chapter 13

Belle Cardwell was somewhere between thirty-five and forty, Longarm guessed once he had lit the lamp in his room and gotten a good look at her. Despite the unmistakable signs of a hard-lived life—the lines around the mouth, a certain coarsening of the skin, the cool certainty in the eyes that most of the time the world was not a good place—she was still attractive. Her figure was good in the dark blue gown she wore. Her dark hair, put up in an elaborate arrangement of curls underneath a matching hat, had only a few strands of gray in it. She reminded Longarm of the madam of a successful cathouse who was a former soiled dove herself.

Either that, or a woman who had latched on to a rich man who was paying quite well to keep her as his mistress.

"I still ain't quite sure why you came to see me tonight," Longarm said as he tossed his hat on the bed. He thought about offering the woman a drink, but he decided to hold off on that for the time being.

"I was in the courtroom today to listen to your testimony," Belle said. "You're a very impressive man, Marshal. The jury paid close attention to you."

"I don't recollect seeing you among the spectators."

"I can make myself appear . . . less noticeable, shall we say? . . . whenever I want to. I assure you, I was there."

"Why?"

"Excuse me?"

"If you're who you say you are, why'd you come to the trial?" Longarm knew he sounded overly suspicious, but he didn't care. He had learned over the years not to take things at face value.

Belle had been smiling at him, an easy, practiced smile that Longarm figured didn't mean a whole hell of a lot, but now she became serious. "I wanted to see her," she said.

"Who?"

"You know who. The woman who took Jericho away from me. His so-called wife." Belle's voice dripped with scorn and contempt.

"Estelle Malone," Longarm said.

"That's right. She's every bit the vicious harpy Jericho always said she was."

Longarm rubbed his jaw. Estelle had looked pretty pathetic to him all during the trial, but he supposed Belle had a different point of view. He said, "Malone told you quite a bit about his wife, did he?"

Belle made a half-turn and waved an elegantly gloved hand. "All men talk . . . especially at certain times."

"He told you that his wife knew about you?"

"He said that she suspected, but that she couldn't know for sure. We were very careful, you know, very discreet. We got together only when there was absolutely no chance of Estelle finding out about it."

"Then how did she know?"

Belle's shoulders rose and fell in a slight shrug. "I'm afraid I can't tell you that, Marshal. I suppose that, despite her cold nature, Estelle Malone was still something of a woman, and a woman can sometimes sense when her man has been with someone else, no matter how careful he is."

Everything Belle was saying was feasible enough, Longarm supposed, but she still hadn't convinced him fully. He said, "Even if you're telling the truth, why come to see me tonight?"

Belle faced him squarely, and her eyes were intent on him as she said, "I told you I was in the courtroom today, Marshal. If you had told the jury you were convinced Estelle Malone killed Jericho, the trial would have been over. Nothing that poor little drab of a lady lawyer could do in Estelle's defense would persuade the jury that she isn't guilty. But you stopped short of that."

"Because I don't know that Mrs. Malone killed her husband," Longarm pointed out. "I just know what it looks like."

"My God, isn't that enough?"

"Not for me."

Belle came closer to him. "Marshal, you have to listen to me. I know she killed him. I know *why* she killed him. He was going to divorce her."

Longarm shook his head. "The way I heard it, Malone's wife wouldn't give him a divorce."

"Yes, but he was finally prepared to fight her on it. Until then, he wanted to spare her any ugliness in the courts. He said that he still felt sorry for her, God knows why after she made him so miserable. But he'd finally had all he could stand. Jericho was very well connected, you know. If he wanted a divorce badly enough, he could have gotten one, no matter what Estelle did."

That was probably true, too, Longarm reflected, and if so, it gave Estelle Malone one more reason to have killed her husband. If Malone had reached the end of his rope and was finally determined to get rid of Estelle, no matter what it took . . . if he had told her that, that night . . . Longarm frowned.

"You know I'm right, don't you?" Belle said softly. "I can see it in your eyes, Marshal. You know that she did it."

"I didn't see her stab him," Longarm said stubbornly. "That's the only thing that's going to make me say I *know*."

Belle had moved close enough to him by now so that she could reach out and lay a hand on his arm. "But if you go back to court and testify, tell the jury what I've told you tonight, I know it would make a difference. Estelle would be convicted for sure."

"I've already testified."

"I'll bet that slick-haired prosecuting attorney would recall you if he knew you had new information."

She was right about that, thought Longarm. Abercrombie Creighton would have him back on the stand in a second if he thought it would help secure a conviction in the case.

"If you feel so strong about this, why don't *you* testify?" he asked.

Haltingly, Belle shook her head. "I . . . I can't. I still have hopes of marrying well someday. It would ruin my chances for that if everyone knew I was Jericho's mistress."

"But you wanted me to say that in court," Longarm said.

Her hand tightened on his arm. "Yes, but you could keep my name out of it."

"The judge could make me reveal it if Miss Parmalee objected. Besides, this whole thing is hearsay. She'd object, and the judge would throw out my testimony."

"Not until after the jury had heard it," Belle said with a sly smile. "You know how things like that work, Marshal. The judge can tell the jury to disregard something, and they'll claim that they did, but they never really do. Once they've heard it for themselves, it's with them forever."

She was right. Janice could raise all the objections she wanted to, and Judge Walton could sustain every one of them, but if Longarm got on the stand and testified that he'd talked to Jericho Malone's mistress and been told that Malone was about to force a divorce on his wife, the jury members would never be able to fully disregard that.

Likely it would be the final nail in the coffin of conviction for Estelle Malone.

"What about it, Marshal?" Belle said. "I know you're thinking about it. You're sworn to uphold the law, remember? And your testimony would put a killer behind bars for the rest of her life."

Longarm rubbed his jaw again. For the second night in a row, a pretty woman had come to his room to ask him to put Estelle away for good. Belle Cardwell's motivation was quite different from Natalie Malone's, but the end result would be the same.

"I'll think on it," Longarm said. "That's all I can promise."

"All right," Belle said, not trying to hide her disappointment that she had failed to obtain a commitment from him. "I'm sure once you've turned it over in your mind a few times, you'll see that I'm right. Good night, Marshal." She moved toward the door.

At least she hadn't offered her body in return for his testimony, like Natalie, Longarm thought. Most people would have expected such behavior much more from the mistress than from the supposedly innocent daughter. That just went to prove that folks weren't always all they seemed to be.

And that was a good thing for a lawman to remember, Longarm told himself as Belle Cardwell left his room. Just because somebody said something, it wasn't always true.

He gave her a couple of minutes' head start, then set out to follow her.

He went down the rear stairs of the boardinghouse and circled around to the street in time to see Belle Cardwell getting into a waiting buggy. It wasn't a cab, but rather a private vehicle. Longarm bit back a curse and darted through the shadows. If he'd had a horse, he could have followed the buggy easily, but on foot like this, it would be a challenge.

He was lucky. No sooner had the buggy rattled across

the bridge over Cherry Creek and headed for downtown Denver than a cab pulled up in front of a nearby house to disgorge a portly, obviously drunk gentleman. Before the drunk had time to stumble through the gate in his fence, Longarm reached the cab, tossed a coin up to the driver on the box, and said, "Swing around and light a shuck for downtown." He pulled himself into the cab and settled back against the seat.

Taking off his hat, he leaned his head out the window and searched for the buggy that had carried away Belle Cardwell. He thought he spotted it, several blocks ahead. The driver of the cab he was in was skillful, handling the matched pair of horses quite well. And at this time of night, there wasn't much traffic. They passed a couple of riders on horseback, but that was all.

The buggy didn't go all the way downtown. It turned into a side street and entered a neighborhood of neat residences. This wasn't the richest part of Denver, but it was far from the poorest. Longarm called to his driver to turn into the side street as well, then stop.

As he dropped from the cab, he clapped his hat back on and peered through the shadows. The buggy carrying Belle had stopped a block and a half ahead, in front of one of the houses. Longarm moved so that the cab obscured him from Belle's view as she climbed down from the buggy. He wondered if she had driven it herself. He was inclined to think so, because she tied the reins of the single horse to a hitching post and left the vehicle there.

Longarm flipped another coin to his driver and muttered, "Much obliged."

"Followin' the lady, mister?" the driver asked.

"I reckon that ain't none of your business," Longarm said curtly.

"No offense. I was just gonna say I'm sorry if you find out something you didn't want to."

On the contrary, Longarm very much wanted to find out what Belle Cardwell was doing here. The house she was approaching might belong to her, but he doubted it.

If she lived here, she probably would have put the buggy and the horse away, rather than leaving them on the street as she had. If she was visiting someone, as seemed much more likely to Longarm, he wanted to know who it was.

He moved into the shadows of the trees that lined the street as Belle went up onto the porch of the house where she had stopped. Longarm's lengthy strides carried him quickly down the street until he was opposite the house. He was close enough to hear Belle rapping insistently on the door. So this was definitely not her home.

The house was dark, but after a moment a yellow glow lit up the front windows. Someone inside had lit a lamp. After another moment, the front door was opened, and the light from inside silhouetted the man who stood there. Instantly, something about him struck Longarm as familiar. The man was short and rather stocky, and the light reflected off his balding head.

Longarm heard Belle's voice but couldn't make out the words. The man stepped back and moved aside to usher her into the house. As he turned, the light fell on his face, and Longarm's eyes narrowed as he recognized Howard Summerlin.

So the late Jericho Malone's mistress was having some sort of rendezvous with his private secretary, who also happened to be the man who had taken over Malone's business affairs after the mining magnate's death. That was interesting, thought Longarm, damned interesting.

Summerlin shut the door. Longarm went closer to the house, moving with a catlike grace unusual in a man with such a rangy, powerful form. He grimaced as, a couple of houses away, a dog started barking. He hoped the yapping pooch wouldn't draw the attention of Summerlin and Belle Cardwell. He wanted to get close enough to the house so that he might be able to hear what was going on.

The light in the front room went out. Longarm paused. He waited until a light appeared in one of the windows on the second floor of the house. That was going to make things more difficult. But there was a tree growing fairly near that side of the house.

As a boy back in West-by-God Virginia, Longarm had climbed plenty of trees, but he hadn't had much call to do so since he'd grown up and come west. Still, some things a fella didn't forget how to do. He stepped over the short fence around the yard and headed toward the tree.

When he reached it, he took off his hat and dropped it on the ground. Then he lifted his arms, glad that his height allowed him to reach the lower branches. Getting a good grip, he braced a foot against the trunk of the tree and pulled himself up. He let go with one hand, reached higher, pulled up again until he could get a foot in the crook of a branch.

Just like being a kid again, he told himself with a faint grin.

Moving slowly and carefully so that he wouldn't cause the leaves to rustle too much, he climbed several more feet, until his head was roughly on a level with the second-floor window where the light was shining. The shade was down, but the window itself was up because the night was warm and full of fragrant breezes.

Longarm tilted his head toward the window and listened intently. What he heard surprised him.

"Oh, yes . . . oh, yes . . . what are you . . . oh, my God! Yes!"

That was Howard Summerlin's voice, all right, thought Longarm, and the words were accompanied by the unmistakable squeaking of bedsprings.

That little son of a bitch. He and Belle Cardwell were going at it like a pair of minks.

Longarm was pondering what that might mean when the branch he was standing on broke under his weight with a loud crack and sent him plummeting toward the ground.

Chapter 14

Longarm reacted instinctively, throwing his arms out wide. He fell only a couple of feet before he was able to grab a branch with his left hand. He dangled there for a second, holding on one-handed, then got his other hand on the branch and scrabbled with his feet for a toehold against the trunk. He found one and braced himself, hoping that Howard Summerlin and Belle Cardwell had been so caught up in their lovemaking that they hadn't heard the crack of the branch.

After a moment, he heard the gasps and cries of passion still coming from inside the room and knew that he had been fortunate. His near-disaster had turned out not so bad after all. Still, he couldn't risk climbing back up there. He went down instead, dropping lightly to the ground a couple of moments later.

He had picked up a couple of stinging scratches on his hands and face during his brief fall, and his left shoulder ached from the weight that had tugged on it when he caught himself. He rolled his shoulder and rotated his arm, deciding that the joint was going to be all right, probably just a little sore for a few days.

He retrieved his hat, then went back to the street, leaving Summerlin and Belle to what they were doing. The cab he'd ridden in earlier was gone, but he didn't mind. The walk back to his room wouldn't hurt him. In fact, he thought, it would give him time to ponder the situation.

When he was several blocks away, he took out a cheroot and lit it so that he could smoke as he walked and thought. The fact that Summerlin and Belle were obviously close made everything she had told him tonight suspect. Was it possible that Belle had been carrying on not only with Jericho Malone but with Malone's secretary as well?

Longarm didn't think that was likely. Any gal who had latched onto Malone wouldn't risk that relationship by fooling around with Summerlin, too. But if Belle was actually Summerlin's mistress instead of Malone's, that meant she had been lying to Longarm tonight. What reason would she have to lie in order to make sure that Estelle was convicted for Malone's murder?

That was easy, Longarm told himself. She was trying to protect the real killer—Howard Summerlin.

He puffed on the cheroot and thought that it had probably been Summerlin's idea for Belle to come see him. Summerlin could have told her everything that had happened in the courtroom that day and coached her in what she was supposed to say to the lawman. The more Longarm turned it over in his head, the more the pieces seemed to fit together.

Unfortunately, Belle's lies didn't prove Estelle's innocence any more than the circumstances of Malone's death proved her guilt. Longarm knew that if he went to Abercrombie Creighton with his suspicions, the prosecuting attorney would just laugh at him. He had to have something else, at least a concrete motive. Sure, Summerlin had taken over the management of Malone's business affairs, but was that enough to justify murder?

Longarm stopped short as a thought occurred to him. He hadn't been looking at the whole thing from a wide enough angle. The murder had taken place here in Denver, but the source of Malone's wealth was somewhere else.

The Colorado Star mine.

Longarm turned around and walked toward downtown instead of back toward his room. He went to the hotel where Janice Parmalee was staying and paused in the lobby to take out his watch. A little after ten o'clock, he saw when he checked the time. It was late, but maybe not too late.

He hadn't taken her up to her room after they dined the night before, but he knew the number. He climbed to the third floor, where the room was located, and found the door. His knuckles rapped softly but insistently on the panel. After a moment, Janice's worried voice sounded, asking, "Who is it?"

"Custis Long," Longarm replied.

The key turned in the lock and the door opened a few inches. Janice peered out at him in confusion. "Marshal Long?" she said. "What is it? What are you doing here?"

He could see only a narrow strip of her body, but that was enough for him to tell that she was clad in a silk dressing gown. Her hair was loose around her shoulders, and it looked lighter and prettier that way. She might not possess the classical beauty of a Natalie Malone, but Janice Parmalee was one of the most purely pretty girls Longarm had ever seen.

He reminded himself why he was there. He took off his hat and said, "Pardon me for intrudin' on your privacy and coming here so late, Miss Parmalee, but I need to talk to you."

"Is it about the Malone case?" she asked.

"That's right."

Janice shook her head. "I'm not sure that's a good idea. After all, you're a witness for the prosecution—"

"Not anymore," Longarm broke in. "Creighton said he was through with me."

"Subject to re-call."

"If he re-calls me, it'll have to be as a hostile witness, because I don't think Estelle Malone killed her husband."

That was the first time he had actually put the feeling

into words, but as he said them, he had the undeniable sense that they were right. He no longer believed that Estelle had killed her husband. In fact, he was more convinced of her innocence than he had ever been of her guilt.

For a moment, Janice stared through the narrow aperture at him, then stepped back and opened the door wider. "Come in," she said.

Longarm stepped into the room, carrying his hat. Janice closed the door behind him. "I'm sorry if this is a mite awkward, havin' me in your room like this—"

"Don't worry about that, Marshal," Janice said. "I don't live here in Denver. I don't have a reputation to protect. Besides, most people seem to have a hard time thinking of me as a brazen hussy, no matter what I do."

And most people didn't have any idea what a lovely young woman she really was, either, thought Longarm. He changed the subject momentarily by asking, "How's your father?"

A smile lit up Janice's face and made her even prettier. "He woke up this afternoon," she said. "Isn't that wonderful? The doctor says he's going to need a great deal of rest, but he's probably going to be all right."

"I'm mighty glad to hear that. I reckon you'll keep on handling the trial, though?"

"Of course. Father may never set foot in a courtroom again, not if he wants to avoid another attack."

Longarm nodded. "What happened today after I testified?"

Janice told him to have a seat in the room's lone armchair, while she sat on the edge of the bed. "Mr. Creighton called Daniel Hubbard, the policeman who investigated Mr. Malone's death."

"I've got a pretty good idea what Dan must've said, since I was there for his part that night."

Janice nodded. "Yes, it was quite damning for Mrs. Malone. Creighton was able to get Mr. Hubbard to say that he thought Mrs. Malone was guilty."

"I know Dan. If he said that, he believes it. He's a good man."

"He doesn't have your skepticism," Janice said. "He was ready to convict Mrs. Malone just because it appears she's the most likely suspect."

"That's the way the law works most of the time, isn't it?"

Janice shrugged her slim shoulders. "Yes, of course. The law says that a person has to be guilty beyond a reasonable doubt, not beyond any doubt at all. If that was the standard of proof, hardly anyone would ever be convicted."

"What about after that?"

"I took a page from your book," Janice said with a smile. "I asked Mr. Hubbard about other suspects, namely Howard Summerlin. Mr. Hubbard said that Summerlin had been investigated and that there was nothing to indicate that he might have had a reason to kill Mr. Malone."

"What about the Colorado Star?"

Janice frowned. "The Colorado Star? The mine that Mr. Malone owned?"

"That's right. Did Hubbard go up there and ask any questions?"

"Well . . . he didn't say anything about it."

Longarm shook his head. "I'd be willin' to bet that he didn't. He probably just asked folks here in town who had business dealings with Malone."

Janice leaned forward and asked, "Are you saying that you suspect Mr. Summerlin even more than before?"

Longarm found that he wasn't willing to reveal everything he had discovered, not until he had something stronger than a hunch. "I'm saying that I'd sure like to poke around a mite and see how that mine's been operating."

"Can you do that? In your capacity as a federal marshal, I mean?"

"Not really." He grinned. "But there's nothing stopping

me from takin' a ride up there as a private citizen."

Janice regarded him with wide hazel eyes. "You'd do that?"

"I'm thinkin' mighty serious on it." Longarm scratched his jaw. "What else happened in court today?"

"Mr. Creighton rested the state's case. That was the last thing before Judge Walton adjourned court until tomorrow."

"Tomorrow's Friday," Longarm mused. "You'll start presenting your case in the morning?"

"That's right."

"Can you stall for a day, call some witnesses who don't really amount to much, and give me until next Monday to do some pokin' around?"

"Well . . . I suppose so. I'd planned to call some people who were acquainted with both Mr. and Mrs. Malone, society friends and such. They won't be very sympathetic to Mrs. Malone, but they'll have to testify that the Malones got along well in public and that there was never any evidence of violence on the part of Mrs. Malone."

"Creighton's already stipulated to that," Longarm reminded her.

"Yes, but he can't stop me from presenting character witnesses. It's all in the way I couch the questions." She smiled. "So, yes, I think I can safely say that I can waste a day and give you tomorrow and the weekend."

"All right." Longarm came to his feet. "I'll try to get back by Sunday evening, at the latest. I'll come see you here and let you know what I find out."

"That would be wonderful, Marshal," Janice said as she stood up. She started to take a step toward him, then stopped, rather awkwardly.

Longarm turned his hat over in his hands. "I ain't promising that I'll come up with anything to clear Mrs. Malone."

"I know that. But it's just such a relief to know that there's someone else in this town who thinks she's innocent." Janice drew in a deep breath, and Longarm could see in her eyes the strain she had been under, dealing not only with her father's illness but with a seemingly impossible legal case at the same time. "Thank you, Marshal."

"You're welcome. I just want to see justice done." He grinned. "Reckon it's a bad habit of mine."

Chapter 15

Longarm started early the next morning, renting a horse from one of the local livery stables and riding southwest out of Denver toward the Front Range of the Rockies. He knew roughly where the Colorado Star mine was located, knew as well that it would take him most of the day to reach it. The nearest settlement was a small town called Harkerville. Longarm hoped to talk to the local lawman there, as well as to the foreman of the Colorado Star.

It was a beautiful morning, with just a hint of coolness in the thin, clear air. A few puffy white clouds floated high overhead in the blue sky. Longarm inhaled deeply, glad to be out of the stuffy courtroom for a change, glad as well to be wearing range clothes again instead of a suit.

As far as Billy Vail was concerned, Longarm was still attending the trial of Estelle Malone. The only problem that might crop up was if Vail happened to talk to Abercrombie Creighton and learn that Longarm hadn't been anywhere near the courthouse today. Even then, Billy couldn't get too mad, thought Longarm. After all, Vail had specifically said he was relieved of his duties as a deputy marshal until after the trial was over.

By midday, Longarm was in the mountains, following the road that led up and over the passes and on to Harkerville. The horse he had chosen at the livery stable had plenty of stamina and an easy, ground-eating gait, even on the slopes. Longarm made better time than he'd expected, arriving in the settlement while there were still a couple of hours of daylight left.

He'd been to Harkerville before, his work having taken him there on several occasions. It was a nice little town nestled in a valley between a couple of towering peaks. Longarm recalled where the sheriff's office was and headed straight there. He got a surprise, though, when he reined up in front of the blocky building made of stone and thick wooden beams. The sign over the door read "Harold Davis—Sheriff."

Longarm wondered what had happened to Al Conroy, who had been sheriff here the last time Longarm had passed through these parts. He swung down from the saddle, looped the horse's reins over the hitchrack, and stepped up onto the office porch. He opened the door and went inside.

A lean man with a shock of thick white hair sat behind the desk. He wore a striped shirt with leather cuffs and a cowhide vest. A tin star was pinned to the vest. "Be with you in a minute, mister," he said without looking up from the newspaper he was reading.

"Sheriff Davis?" asked Longarm.

"That's right." The local lawman folded the paper and tossed it onto the desk. "What can I do for you?"

"I'm Custis Long, deputy U.S. marshal out of Denver."

Davis sat up straighter. "The one they call Longarm?"

"Sometimes," Longarm admitted with a shrug.

Davis stood up and extended a hand across the desk. "Well, I'm glad to meet you, Marshal. Sheriff Conroy told me about how he'd worked with you a couple of times. Said you were one hell of a lawman."

Longarm smiled and shook hands with the sheriff. "Glad to hear Al had such a high opinion of me, whether it's justified or not. What happened to him? Nothing bad, I hope."

"Not unless you consider retirement a bad thing," Davis said with a smile of his own. "The old hell-raiser headed out to California to live with his daughter and her family."

Longarm chuckled. "Sounds like you know Al pretty well."

"We deputied together up in the Dakotas, a long time ago. When he decided to hang up his badge, he wired me about the job, said I might like to put in for it. I was working as a constable back in Wichita." A broad grin stretched across Davis's leathery face. "I like it here a lot better. I never was much of a flatlander." Davis gestured toward a potbellied iron stove in a corner of the office. "Coffee?"

"Don't mind if I do," said Longarm.

"You up here on business, Marshal?" Davis asked as he poured two cups of coffee from the battered old pot staying warm on the stove.

"I reckon you could say I'm conducting an unofficial investigation. It has to do with the Colorado Star mine."

Davis frowned. "You mean Uncle Sam's finally taking an interest in those robberies?"

If Longarm had been a dog, his ears would have perked up at that. "Robberies?" he repeated.

"Yeah, the Colorado Star has lost several shipments of silver lately. The mine is in the mountains, about five miles west of here, so they have to bring the silver here by wagon to load it on the train that runs on our narrow-gauge spur line. Only the past few months, owlhoots have been hitting the wagons."

To give himself time to turn that information over in his mind, Longarm took a sip of the coffee in the cup that Davis handed him. It was black and damned near strong enough to get up and walk off by itself—just the way Longarm liked it.

"The Mint buys a lot of silver for coins," he finally said. "Which means the government don't take kindly to anything that disrupts the flow of it."

He was just giving himself an excuse for the poking

around he intended to do, but the odd thing about it was that if the Colorado Star was losing silver shipments as Sheriff Davis indicated, that might indeed be a legitimate reason for him to investigate. Maybe he wasn't as far out on a limb as he'd thought he was.

"Well, I've tried to track down that gang," Davis said with a heavy sigh, "but I haven't had a bit of luck. They're slippery devils, and they always seem to know when a shipment's going out from the mine, even though Ben Jeppson, the foreman, tries to fool them."

"How's he do that?" Longarm asked.

"Decoy wagons, taking different routes, things like that. None of it seems to do any good." Davis's face became grim as he went on, "Three guards have been killed and several more shot up pretty bad during those robberies. I'd sure like to get my hands on whoever is responsible for them. If that's why you're up here, Marshal, I'll sure give you a hand any way I can."

"I'm obliged for the offer, and I'll take you up on it. I need to ride out to the mine and talk to Jeppson. Reckon you could show me the way?"

"Damn right. Finish up your coffee, and I'll go saddle my horse."

Ten minutes later, the two men rode out of Harkerville, headed west. The road was now little more than a trail, barely wide enough for a wagon. It wound through valleys and over passes, following a fast-flowing creek part of the way. The water was white with froth as it rippled and bubbled over the rocks in the streambed. Longarm spotted several deer and even an elk. It was hard to believe this almost pristine wilderness was less than a day's ride from Denver.

Not all the landscape was untouched, however, he discovered as they followed the trail around a bend and saw several buildings and a dark gaping hole in the side of the mountain at the far end of a little valley.

"That's the Colorado Star," Sheriff Davis explained. "There are a couple of other mines in the area, but the

Star's the only one that's really paid off. Jericho Malone started working the claim over twenty years ago, from what I've heard. I wasn't around here then, of course. You hear that Malone got himself killed, down there in Denver?"

"I heard something about it," Longarm said.

Davis shook his head. "Bad business. Wife stabbed him, if I recollect right."

"So they say." Longarm didn't mention that Estelle Malone's trial was going on right now—although with any luck, Janice's stalling tactics had made sure it was an unproductive day in the courtroom.

"Just goes to show you that money can't buy you love," mused Davis as he and Longarm rode toward the mine. "Nor save you if somebody sticks a knife in your gizzard."

"That's the truth," Longarm agreed.

The sun was already dipping behind the mountains to the west. It would be well after dark by the time the two men got back to Harkerville. Davis seemed to know the trail, though, so Longarm wasn't worried about being able to return to the settlement. Shadows gathered as they started up the slope toward the buildings of the mine compound.

The largest building was long and narrow, obviously a barracks for the miners. Longarm saw a couple of storage sheds, a stamp mill, an office building, a small cottage where the mine foreman probably lived, and off to one side by itself, a small, rugged stone structure that had to be the magazine where the blasting powder was kept. The stamp mill was running, a low rumble coming from its machinery, but Longarm didn't see anybody around. The miners were probably all down in the shaft itself.

As he and Davis drew rein in front of the office building, the door opened and a man stepped out onto the porch. He was a tall, rawboned individual in lace-up boots, jeans, and a red-checked flannel shirt. He lifted a hand in greeting and said, "I thought I saw somebody coming. Howdy, Sheriff."

"Ben," Davis said with a friendly nod. He crossed his hands on his saddle horn and leaned forward, inclining his head toward Longarm. "This here is Marshal Custis Long, from Denver. He's a federal lawman, come to investigate those robberies that have been plaguing you."

A look of pleased surprise came over Ben Jeppson's face. He said, "A federal lawman? Really? Come on in, Marshal. You, too, Sheriff."

Longarm and Davis dismounted, tethered their mounts to one of the porch posts, and climbed the short flight of steps. Jeppson ushered them inside and offered them coffee from a pot that was almost a twin of the one in Davis's office. The room was cluttered, but Jeppson made room for Longarm and Davis to sit on an old sofa. He went behind a scarred wooden desk and sat down in a ladder-back chair.

"I'm mighty glad to see you, Marshal," Jeppson said. "I figured Uncle Sam would take an interest in our problems sooner or later."

Longarm didn't tell the mine foreman that the robberies hadn't actually come to the attention of the government. Instead he said, "Tell me about what's been going on up here."

"Sure. You know we stamp the ore into bars here?"

Longarm nodded. "I saw the mill."

"Once we've done that, we load the bars onto wagons and take them down to Harkerville to put them on the train into Denver."

"I told the marshal about that," Davis put in.

"We never had any trouble until lately," Jeppson went on. "Then, within the last six months or so, our wagons started getting hit by holdup men. After the first time, I put more guards on the job, but it didn't do any good." Jeppson's mouth quirked bitterly. "All it did was get some good men killed."

Longarm said, "Surely they don't hit every shipment?"

Jeppson shook his head. "No. There have been seven robberies so far. Some of the shipments have gotten through without any trouble." He paused, then added meaningfully, "The smaller shipments."

"You mean it's the big shipments that get held up?"

"That's right."

Longarm took out a cheroot and turned it over in his fingers as he thought. "Sounds to me like those owlhoots know when the big shipments are going out."

Davis grunted. "That's what I thought, too. Especially after Ben started tryin' to mix 'em up."

"That didn't help, either," Jeppson said. "I sent out decoys, had the wagons use different trails that go the long way around to town, started them in the middle of the night . . . Nothing did any good. The outlaws still got the silver."

"Sure sounds like an inside job," said Longarm. "You got anybody up here you're suspicious of?"

Jeppson shook his head. "Most of the men have been here for a long time. They're loyal workers."

"Meanin' no offense, Jeppson," Longarm said slowly, "but how long have *you* worked here?"

Jeppson's eyes narrowed for a moment, then he relaxed and chuckled. "Guess I can't blame a man for being suspicious when that's his job. I've been part of this operation for over ten years, Marshal. Started out as a mucker down in the shaft. So I guess you could say I've worked my way up to foreman, and when I say up, I mean up."

"Like I said, no offense meant." Longarm hesitated, then went on, "I reckon you know about Mr. Malone?"

"About him being killed? Sure, we heard all about it. His wife stabbed him."

"That's what they say," muttered Longarm. "Has Malone's death affected things up here?"

Jeppson shook his head. "Not much. We all know that Mr. Malone's heirs will want to keep the mine working. Mr. Summerlin told me just to keep on like we've been doing."

"That'd be Howard Summerlin, Malone's secretary?" Longarm kept his voice carefully neutral.

"That's right. He's the one running things now, I suppose, until it all gets sorted out."

"Been up here a lot, has he?"

"Quite a few times, especially since Mr. Malone died. Of course, he came up pretty often before that, checking up on things for Mr. Malone. I guess that was part of his job."

Longarm nodded, still not allowing his expression to betray what he was thinking.

If Howard Summerlin was intimately familiar with the mine's operation, it stood to reason that he would probably know about the robberies that had been going on. And yet, he had said nothing about them to Longarm or anyone else who had investigated Jericho Malone's murder. It was also reasonable to assume that Summerlin would be privy to the details of the silver shipments leaving the mine bound for Harkerville. If Summerlin had been passing along that information to somebody else, say a gang of owlhoots operating in the area . . .

It looked to Longarm like he had sure enough found a motive for murder, especially if Malone had discovered somehow what Summerlin was doing.

"Well, what do you think, Marshal?" Jeppson was saying. "Do you figure you can put a stop to the robberies?"

"I'd sure like to," Longarm said. What he really wanted was to get his hands on some of those outlaws and see if he could make them talk.

"Then I reckon you'll be spending the night?"

Longarm frowned in surprise. "Why's that?"

"There's a big shipment leaving here first thing in the morning. I just reckoned you knew about it and intended to go along."

Longarm only had to think about it for a second before he nodded and said, "Yep, that's exactly what I plan to do."

Chapter 16

There were three wagons in the convoy, each of them loaded with silver ingots which were then covered with a tied-down canvas tarpaulin. Two men rode on the box of each wagon, a driver and a guard. The guard carried a Winchester and packed a pair of six-guns, while the driver rode with his foot on a scattergun that would be handy to snatch up in case of trouble.

Six outriders completed the party—one in front, two on each flank, and one bringing up the rear. All of them carried Winchesters. It was a pretty formidable group, Longarm thought as he looked them over the next morning in the predawn light. A dozen men, all of them armed. Even if the outlaws had been tipped off, it wouldn't be easy to stop this shipment from getting through to Harkerville.

Sheriff Davis had returned to the settlement the previous night, after having supper with Longarm and Jeppson. Longarm had bedded down for the night on the sofa in the mine foreman's office. It wasn't the most comfortable bed he'd ever had, but he had slept in a lot worse places.

As the convoy assembled in front of the storage sheds, Jeppson said to Longarm, "Do you want to ride on one of the wagons, Marshal?"

Longarm shook his head. "Nope. In fact, I plan to follow along on horseback and stay out of sight for the most part."

"How's that going to stop that gang from holding up the wagons?" Jeppson asked with a frown.

"One man more or less ain't going to stop them from making a try for the silver," Longarm explained. "What I want to do is be in position to spoil things for them if they do hit the wagons."

Jeppson nodded slowly. "I reckon you know best, Marshal."

Longarm had brought his own Winchester with him, and he hefted the rifle now and said, "Don't worry. If those owlhoots show up, they'll be in for a surprise."

Jeppson grinned. "I'm tempted to go with you, Marshal. I think I'd like to see that."

Longarm shook his head and said, "I'd rather you stay right here and carry on like usual."

Jeppson lowered his voice so that only Longarm could hear him. "If somebody here *is* working with the outlaws, they've seen you and likely know that you're a lawman."

"That's why it's up to you to keep an eye on everybody. If anybody tries to slip off—like to warn the gang—you grab 'em and hang on to 'em until I get back."

"I'll sure do that," Jeppson agreed with an emphatic nod.

Longarm didn't think that was going to happen, but at least he had that angle covered now. Casually, he asked, "When was the last time Howard Summerlin was up here?"

"About a week ago," replied Jeppson. "He's been around even more since Mr. Malone died. Guess he feels like he has to watch out for the estate's interests."

The answer didn't surprise Longarm. He knew Summerlin had been in Denver for the trial of Estelle Malone. But it was worrisome in another way.

"Then he doesn't know about this shipment?"

"Actually, he does. When I planned it out, I sent a letter

to him in town so he'd know. Sent it by a special rider, so it'd get there in plenty of time. Mr. Summerlin really likes to stay on top of things."

Including Belle Cardwell, thought Longarm. He wondered which of that pair had actually come up with the idea of robbing the silver shipments from the Colorado Star.

He would find out sooner or later, he told himself grimly. All he needed was some leverage, and either of those two would crack wide open. Maybe today would provide him with what he needed to know.

The day's work was getting under way down below, in the stopes and galleries of the mine, as up above the three wagons pulled out with their valuable cargoes. Longarm let them get a lead, then shook hands with Ben Jeppson and swung up into his saddle. The horse had spent the night in the crude stable where the mule teams were kept. It pranced along, eager to be out and about again on this cool mountain morning.

Longarm's job had taken him all over these mountains at one time or another, so he had no trouble following the convoy while still staying out of sight of the wagons. He veered off the main trail onto a smaller one and followed it higher into the peaks. From time to time, as he wound through the mountains, he caught sight of the wagons far below him. His eyes constantly searched the rugged terrain around him, looking for any warning signs of trouble. If the outlaws hit the wagons, they would probably have some sort of ambush set up. Longarm hoped he was high enough so that if that happened, he could bushwhack the bushwhackers.

The sun rose and climbed higher in the deep blue sky above the snowcapped crags. The morning grew warmer, and after an hour or so Longarm took off his denim jacket and draped it over the saddle in front of him. Jeppson had said that the wagons would take most of the morning to cover the five miles to Harkerville. They had to take it slow and easy on the narrow, winding trail. There were a few places where, if a wheel slipped, a wagon might topple right off the trail and go rolling down a steep slope. The drivers were all experienced men, however, and knew how to handle the vehicles and the mules pulling them.

Longarm estimated the convoy had covered at least two-thirds of the distance to the settlement when he began to wonder if nothing was going to happen. It was possible the gang would pass on this opportunity. Or maybe Summerlin hadn't received word of it in time to set up another robbery. Longarm chewed on an unlit cheroot as his emotions warred inside of him. He wanted to break this case open, but at the same time, he couldn't wish an ambush on the men with the wagons. That would just put them in danger . . .

The sudden cracking of rifle shots told him that he wouldn't have to ponder the situation any longer. It was out of his hands now.

He spurred ahead, drawing rein at the edge of a bluff that gave him a good view of what was happening down below. This was one of those places where the main trail was even narrower than usual, so that the outriders had to pull in and ride close beside the wagons. The slope fell off steeply to the left and rose almost as steeply on the right. A band of pine trees grew across the mountainside above the trail, and puffs of smoke came from those trees now as men hidden there opened fire on the wagons. The guards and the outriders returned the fire, but as Longarm watched grimly, he saw one of the riders pitch from the saddle and fall to the ground in the limp sprawl that signified death.

The drivers whipped up their teams and shouted at the mules, trying to goad them into a faster pace. Before the mules could take off, however, a boulder came tumbling and bounding down the slope, dislodged from its previous precarious perch by the bandits. It was headed straight for the lead wagon. The driver and the guard saw it coming, yelled in fear, and leaped off the wagon box just in time to escape the crunching collision as the boulder struck the wagon. The side boards splintered under the impact, and some of the piled-up ingots in the wagon bed were knocked loose to slither out onto the ground. The wagon itself lifted into the air on its right side and toppled over. Longarm expected it to go tumbling down the slope, pulling the frantically braying mule team with it, but somehow it came to rest on its side, just below the trail, and stayed there. The mules were tangled in their harness and some of them had fallen. They kicked and struggled futilely.

The shooting was still going on as the guards and outriders did their best to fight off the attack. Longarm couldn't see the outlaws, but he figured they probably outnumbered the defenders. Even if they didn't, they held the high ground and a decided advantage.

Or so they thought.

Longarm levered a shell into the chamber of the borrowed Winchester, then gripped the rifle in his right hand while he took the reins tightly in his left. "Come on, old son," he said to the horse. "It's time we took a hand in this."

With that he urged the horse over the edge of the bluff. The animal was reluctant at first, but then, as gravity took over, it had no choice except to go along. It stiffened its forelegs, lowered its rear end, and began sliding and crow-hopping down the mountainside.

That made the saddle even more of a hurricane deck than normal. Longarm didn't expect to be able to hit anything, but he knew he had to distract the outlaws. He fired the rifle one-handed toward the trees. The Winchester's heavy recoil kicked it up. Longarm used the recoil to allow him to cock the weapon one-handed, then he fired again.

His bullets must have come close enough to the owlhoots to alert them that they were being attacked from behind, because a slug suddenly kicked up dust from the rocky slope to his right. He saw a muzzle flash in the shadows under the pines and heard the all-too-familiar flat *whap!* of a bullet disturbing the air close to his head. He was within fifty yards of the trees now, so he dropped the reins, kicked his feet free of the stirrups, and pitched out of the saddle, holding tightly to the Winchester. He couldn't afford to lose it when he landed.

A second later he slammed hard into the ground and rolled over a couple of times, coming to a stop behind the cluster of rocks that had looked like the most likely cover to him. A few yards downslope, the horse was struggling to stay upright. The sudden departure of Longarm's weight from its back had thrown the animal off balance. It recovered, though, and without Longarm to urge it on, trotted off to one side. Longarm was glad the horse hadn't fallen; that would have most likely meant a broken leg and death for the animal.

Meanwhile, Longarm had problems of his own, most notably the outlaw bullets whipping around him. Firing uphill was difficult. Most of the shots went well over Longarm's head. But aiming downhill was hard, too. He slid the barrel of the Winchester over the top of a rock and triggered a couple of shots. Both of them kicked up dust and splinters of rock upslope from the pines, he saw to his disgust. He was trying to adjust his aim when a bullet hit the rock only a few inches from his ear and made him duck.

Down below on the main trail, the outriders had dismounted and joined the drivers and guards behind the cover of the wagons. The piled-up ingots of silver made a good barricade, and the men began peppering the trees with gunfire. Longarm got off three more shots from above and was rewarded with the sight of a man falling from behind one of the tree trunks. Now that he was getting the range, he raised himself a little more and poured lead down on the trees, firing as fast as he could jack fresh cartridges into the Winchester's chamber. A cloud of powdersmoke floated in the air around him.

The would-be silver thieves were unexpectedly caught between two fires, and after a couple of minutes, they broke and ran. Longarm saw several men dart from the shelter of the trees and into a coulee that ran around the side of the mountain. He snapped a shot after them but didn't think he hit any of them as they disappeared. Their horses were probably hidden somewhere around there, he thought. A moment later, the rapid clatter of fleeing hoofbeats confirmed the guess.

Longarm didn't know if all the outlaws had taken off for the tall and uncut or not. He hoped they hadn't, because he still wanted to capture at least one of them. He risked drawing their fire in order to find out, scrambling from behind the cover of the rocks and into the open. Sure enough, a gun cracked and something plucked at the sleeve of Longarm's shirt. He rolled to the side and came upright, digging the low heels of his boots into the ground to keep his balance as he darted lower on the slope, angling toward the pines.

A renewed burst of gunfire came from the men with the wagons, distracting any outlaws who were left. Longarm took advantage of the respite to slide the last few feet into the shelter of the trees, scattering pebbles around him. He took a couple of deep breaths, then called to the men at the wagons, "This is Marshal Long! Hold your fire!"

The shooting died away. Longarm knew he was in this thick band of trees with at least one of the outlaws. From an all-out battle this suddenly had turned into a cat-and-mouse game. He began to work his way forward, ducking from tree to tree, the rifle held ready in his hands.

A shot blasted, and bark leaped away from the trunk of the tree beside which Longarm crouched. He pivoted to the right, snapped the rifle to his shoulder, and fired at the puff of smoke he had seen from the corner of his eye. A man came flying out awkwardly from behind one of the pines, landing hard on his back and twitching. A rifle clattered away from him. Longarm saw crimson spurt from the twitching man's neck and bit back a curse. That jasper would never be able to talk. He would be dead in a matter of seconds. Longarm's bullet had torn his throat out.

He wasn't the only outlaw left, however, as Longarm discovered a second later when a revolver blasted behind him. His hat flew off his head. He dived for the ground, twisting and bringing the Winchester around as he fell. Two men came at him, both of them firing six-guns. Longarm triggered the rifle, and one of the owlhoots doubled over and was thrown backward off his feet as the slug from the Winchester bored into his belly.

Longarm came up off the ground as the hammer of the second man's gun clicked on an empty chamber. The outlaw gasped, "Shit!" He dropped the gun and grabbed for a knife thrust behind his belt as Longarm charged him.

The outlaw had just touched the hilt of the knife when Longarm drove the butt of the Winchester's stock into his jaw. The blow sent the outlaw flying backward. Half-stunned, he still managed to pull the knife while he was lying on the ground. Longarm kicked it out of his hand, levered a fresh cartridge into the Winchester's chamber, and jabbed the muzzle of the rifle against the man's forehead.

"It's over, old son," Longarm told him. "You're under arrest. Now be still, because I'd hate like hell to have to splatter your brains all over the side of this mountain."

Chapter 17

The prisoner admitted reluctantly that his name was Johnny Corben. Some of his reluctance was due to an outlaw's natural aversion to giving his right name, and some of it was because it hurt like hell for him to talk. His jaw was quite bruised and swollen where Longarm had clouted him with the butt of the Winchester.

Longarm cuffed Corben's hands behind his back and prodded him into one of the wagons that was still upright. The one that had been knocked onto its side by the falling boulder had ropes tied to it and was hauled back onto its wheels by some of the mules that were unhitched from the tangled harness. None of the mules were badly hurt, and they would be able to continue pulling the wagon into Harkerville.

The outrider Longarm had seen fall from his horse was dead, all right, drilled through the chest. His companions were furious, and as they cast murderous glances toward Corben, Longarm had to remind them, "This gent is a federal prisoner, boys, and I aim to see that he stays healthy enough to hang."

The words accomplished a dual purpose. They kept the guards and drivers and outriders from lynching or shooting the captured owlhoot here and now, and they reminded Corben that he was facing the gallows for his part in the robbery. Longarm knew there was nothing like the prospect of having his neck stretched to make an hombre decide to talk.

Longarm caught his horse, tied it onto the back of the wagon where Corben rode, and climbed into the vehicle with the outlaw as the convoy got under way again. Longarm sat down on the pile of silver ingots, the borrowed rifle across his knees, and reflected that silver might be a precious metal but it sure as hell didn't make a very comfortable seat. He said to Corben, "Who planned this holdup?"

Corben just regarded him sullenly. "I ain't tellin' you nothin' else, law dog," he said.

Longarm winced. "Did you practice what you'd say if you was ever arrested? If you did, I got to say you could've come up with something better'n that. You and me both know you're going to talk, Corben."

Corben spat over the side of the wagon. "Go to hell."

"You'll be there ahead of me," Longarm told him. "I reckon once I get you back to Denver, it won't take long for you to stand trial and be found guilty. Then you'll be taken to Fort Leavenworth to be hanged." Longarm nodded solemnly. "Yep, you'll be dancin' on air in a month. Six weeks at the most."

Corben paled slightly but maintained his belligerent attitude. He looked away.

Longarm reached over with the Winchester, stuck the barrel under Corben's chin, and pulled the outlaw's head around toward him. "You ever see a man hang?" he asked.

"Go to hell," Corben said again, his voice more strained now because of the pressure of the rifle barrel under his chin.

"The lucky ones, their necks break and they cash in their chips right away," Longarm went on as if he hadn't heard the curse. "It's the ones who strangle to death that are really pathetic to watch. They kick around and swing back and forth while their faces turn blue and then black.

You don't want to be standin' too close if that happens, because they shit themselves and their piss lets go, too. Makes for a bad stink. Sometimes it takes five or ten minutes for them to die." Longarm shook his head. "I reckon that five or ten minutes must seem a heap longer to them."

"Damn it!" Corben burst out into the silence that followed Longarm's words. "What do you want?"

"Who planned that holdup?" Longarm asked again.

"I don't know!"

"I ain't sure I hardly believe that . . ."

"It's the truth, I tell you!" Corben was sweating now. He licked his lips and went on, "One of the men you killed back yonder was Walt Springer. He was the ramrod of our bunch. He gave us our orders."

"Was it his idea to hit those silver shipments? He picked the shipments to rob?"

Corben hesitated, then shrugged. "I don't rightly know. But I don't think so. I think somebody else was tellin' Walt what to do and when to do it. Sometimes he left us at the hideout and rode off for two or three days, and when he came back, he'd tell us about the next job we were goin' to pull."

Longarm nodded. Three days was long enough for the outlaw called Springer to ride to Denver in answer to a summons from Howard Summerlin. "Go on."

Corben licked his lips again. "Sometimes he wasn't gone that long, but he still left and then came back and then we pulled another holdup."

On those occasions, Springer could have met with Summerlin somewhere else, somewhere in the mountains closer to the gang's hideout. It was all coming together just as he had suspected, thought Longarm, but he still didn't have any proof against Summerlin.

"Springer always went by himself when he left the hideout?"

"Yeah. I reckon Walt didn't really trust the rest of us."

"Well, there's that old saying about no honor among thieves," Longarm said.

Corben's mouth twisted in a grimace. "We had plenty of honor. We always done what Walt told us to, no questions asked. And it was a fair split, all the way around."

"Sounds like you had a good thing going."

"Yeah . . . until you had to come along and ruin it all."

"Don't hold your breath waitin' for an apology, old son," Longarm said. "Your bunch killed some good men in those robberies."

Corben shrugged. "They knew the job was dangerous when they took it."

Longarm resisted the impulse to backhand the son of a bitch. He didn't hold with beating up on prisoners . . . but from time to time, under certain circumstances, he was tempted to break that private rule of his.

The convoy rolled on to Harkerville, at a slower pace than usual because of the damage to the lead wagon. By early afternoon, though, the settlement came into sight. The small depot where the silver would be unloaded to wait for the next train to arrive on the spur line was on the far side of the sheriff's office, so Longarm asked the driver to stop in front of the jail as they passed. He climbed down from the wagon bed and untied his horse, then motioned for Corben to get out.

"How can I when I've got my hands cuffed behind my back?" the outlaw whined.

"That's your problem," Longarm told him. "You can figure out a way to manage, or I'll just shoot you and roll your corpse out."

Corben looked like he didn't believe Longarm would actually go that far, but he didn't want to take the chance. He pushed himself to his feet and awkwardly jumped down from the wagon, falling as he hit the ground because he couldn't balance himself properly. As dust puffed up around him, the door of the sheriff's office opened and Harold Davis stepped out. He saw the handcuffed prisoner lying in the street and said with a grin to Longarm, "Looks like you got one of them!"

Longarm transferred the Winchester from right hand to left, then reached down and caught hold of Corben's collar. He hauled the outlaw to his feet and shoved him toward the jail. "Lock him up for me, will you, Sheriff?" Longarm requested. "You have a telegraph office here in town, don't you?"

"We sure do," replied Davis. "Harkerville's all modern and up-to-date."

"Good. I'll wire my boss and tell him I got the mastermind of those silver thieves in custody."

Corben's eyes widened as he stared back at Longarm. "Mastermind!" he yelped. "I told you Walt Springer ran the gang, Marshal! I told you everything you wanted to know!"

Longarm stepped closer to him and said quietly, "Except who was givin' Springer his orders. You think on that, Corben. You think on it long and hard and try to remember anything you might've seen or heard that would put me on the trail of Springer's boss. Otherwise, somebody's got to take the blame for what's been goin' on up here, and it might as well be you."

"But that ain't fair! I never killed nobody! Those guards who were shot, it was other fellas who gunned them down, not me!"

There was a chance Corben was telling the truth. More likely, he had slung lead with the rest of the gang and had no real idea whether his shots had killed anybody or not. But Longarm wanted him kept off balance and worried. He wanted Corben to dredge out even the slightest detail that might help him nail Howard Summerlin for the silver robberies and for Jericho Malone's murder.

Suddenly, Longarm stiffened. He was being just as closed-minded as everybody else, he realized. He had been angry with the police, the prosecution, and everyone else involved in the case for assuming that Estelle Malone was guilty simply because she was the most convenient suspect. And yet here he was, believing that Summerlin was guilty and searching for facts to confirm his theory, rather than simply looking for the truth. He was as big a conclusion-jumper as anybody else, he told himself wryly.

Cautioning himself that he would be better off keeping an open mind, he said to Corben, "You just think on it, old son, and see what you come up with. I'll be by later to talk to you."

Corben looked stricken as he was prodded into the jail by Sheriff Davis. His chances for survival simply as a captured member of the gang weren't all that good to start with. If he was made the scapegoat for the whole thing, he would swing for sure.

Longarm was both dry and hungry. He headed over to the nearest saloon for a dust-cutter, then walked across the street to a hash house and had a late lunch. While he was eating a bowl of stew, Sheriff Davis came into the place, spotted him, and walked over. The sheriff dropped his hat on the table and took one of the empty chairs.

"Got that fella locked up good and tight," he reported. "He won't be going anywhere until we're ready to let him out."

"That jail of yours is pretty solid, I recollect from the last time I was here," Longarm commented.

Davis nodded. "I haven't had anybody bust out, and I don't think Sheriff Conroy did before me, either. That gent ain't really the ringleader of the gang, is he? He don't hardly seem smart enough."

"He's just a second-rate owlhoot who thought he was tough," Longarm replied with a shake of his head. "I can't even prove he killed anybody, though a jury might sentence him to hang anyway, just on general principles. Just as likely to send him off for a few years in the hoosegow, though."

"But you don't want him knowing that," Davis said shrewdly.

"That's right. I want him thinking the hangman's waitin' for him. That way he's more likely to tell me the truth."

Davis regarded him across the table. "I've got a hunch you think you already know what that is."

Longarm thought it over for a moment, then shrugged. He trusted the sheriff, and it might not hurt to trot his theory past somebody else and see if they agreed.

"I think I know who the inside man is who's been tipping off the gang about the silver shipments."

Davis leaned forward and lowered his voice. "Ben Jeppson? Because I can't hardly believe that, Marshal."

"Neither do I," said Longarm. "I think it's Howard Summerlin."

"Who?" Davis frowned. "You mean that little fella who looks after Jericho Malone's business dealin's?"

"He had just as much opportunity to kill Malone as Mrs. Malone did, and if he was mixed up with the robberies and Malone somehow found out about it, that would sure give him a motive, wouldn't it?"

Davis's eyes had grown wider as Longarm spoke. "Wait just a doggone minute," he said. "We were talkin' about the holdups, and now you go to talkin' about murder instead."

"I'm convinced Summerlin's guilty of both. I think he and a ladyfriend of his are trying to frame Mrs. Malone for the killing." Quickly, Longarm sketched in the details of the case for the sheriff. At first, Davis looked pretty skeptical, but as Longarm talked, uncertainty appeared on the face of the local lawman. By the time Longarm was finished, Davis was nodding slowly and looking halfway convinced.

"It sure could've been that way, I suppose. But how are you going to prove any of it?"

Longarm laughed humorlessly. "That's the problem, all right."

"Now, if that outlaw locked up over in the jail had actually *seen* Summerlin, or even talked to him . . ."

"That would do it," Longarm said. "But from what he

told me earlier, Summerlin only met with the gang's ramrod. The rest of the bunch never saw him."

"Maybe the boss outlaw said something to Corben, something that would point toward Summerlin."

That was the slender hope to which Longarm was clinging. He mopped the last of the stew out of the bowl with a piece of cornbread, then washed it down with a swig of buttermilk from the glass beside his plate. He said, "Now that Corben's had some time to think about it, I reckon I ought to go back over there and see if he's remembered anything."

"Sounds like a good idea. Mind some company?"

Longarm grinned. "It's your jail, Sheriff."

The lawmen picked up their hats and headed for the door of the hash house. Longarm paused on the boardwalk outside to slide a cheroot from his shirt pocket. As he lit it, Davis asked, "Got another of those stogies?"

"Sure," Longarm said, reaching for another cheroot.

He had it halfway out of his pocket when the explosion ripped through the peaceful mid-afternoon air and made the planks tremble under his feet. He and Davis both whirled toward the sound of the blast, and the sheriff exclaimed, "Good Lord! That came from the jail!"

Chapter 18

As he broke into a run toward the jail, Longarm saw a cloud of smoke and dust boiling up from behind the squatty stone building. The cell block was located in the rear, and that was where Johnny Corben was locked up.

Longarm jerked his Colt from the cross-draw rig on his left hip as he approached the jail. Sheriff Davis was half a step behind him, and the local lawman had his gun drawn, too. He called to Longarm, "Corben's pards must be tryin' to bust him out!"

That had been Longarm's first thought, too, but as he recalled the sound of the explosion, he wasn't so sure anymore. The blast had seemed louder and more violent than what would be needed to blow down a wall.

The smoke coming from the jail was darker now, telling Longarm that the building was on fire inside. He shouted to Davis, "Take the front! I'll go around back!" He didn't wait to see if Davis was going to argue with that decision or not. He reached the narrow lane alongside the jail and pounded down it toward the alley at the rear.

Before he reached the corner of the building, he heard hoofbeats. There was no time to waste. Throwing caution to the winds, he flung himself around the corner and brought up his revolver.

Two figures on horseback were racing away from the burning jail, galloping toward the wooded slope of the mountain that rose about a quarter of a mile away. Longarm stopped short and thrust his arm out straight, leveling the Colt. The range was almost too great already for a handgun, but he'd left the Winchester inside the sheriff's office. Longarm eared back the hammer on the Colt, steadied the gun by grasping his right wrist with his left hand, and squinted over the sights. He took a deep breath, held it, and gently stroked the trigger.

The forty-five bucked against his palm. He controlled the recoil, brought down the barrel, and fired again, then pivoted slightly and fired twice more, aiming this time at the second of the two fleeing riders.

Those shots missed their mark, Longarm saw as the cloud of powdersmoke around his head thinned and blew away. But the first man he'd aimed at was down, and the man's horse was racing on with an empty saddle. The man Longarm had shot lay motionless on the ground.

Longarm reloaded as he trotted toward the fallen man. He snapped the cylinder shut and paused about ten feet away, just in case the gent was shamming. The man had landed facedown, and judging by the big bloodstain on the back of his shirt, he wasn't going anywhere ever again. Longarm approached with caution, the Colt held ready, and hooked a boot toe under the man's shoulder to roll him over onto his back.

The man was gaunt and unshaven and looked rough as a cob. Longarm had never seen him up close before, but he thought it was highly likely this was one of the outlaws who had gotten away from the ambush on the way into Harkerville. He was dead, all right, his eyes open and glassy as he stared unseeing at the blue afternoon sky. One of Longarm's slugs had bored right through him and burst out of his chest, leaving a fist-sized hole behind.

Longarm glanced toward the mountain. The other rider was out of sight by now, vanished somewhere up there on the thickly wooded slope. Longarm knew that he made a pretty good target, standing out in the open like this, if that hombre wanted to stop running and take a potshot at him with a rifle instead. But Longarm didn't figure that was going to happen. The man hadn't seemed interested in anything except getting away from the scene of the explosion as fast as possible.

As Longarm holstered his gun, he turned away from the dead outlaw and hurried toward the jail. The building was still on fire. Longarm saw now that a hole had indeed been blown in the rear wall, but the damage was extensive in the rest of the building, too. Through the gaping opening, he saw flames leaping and dancing.

Johnny Corben wasn't out here, and he hadn't had time to get away on foot. There had only been two horses, and the second man, the one who had successfully escaped, wasn't Corben. Longarm was sure of that. The second outlaw had been much more heavily built than Corben.

That left only one place the prisoner could be, and that was still inside the burning jail.

Sheriff Davis came around the corner of the building as Longarm approached the scene of destruction. The local lawman was coughing, and his face was grimy with smoke.

"There's no way in from the front," he said, raising his voice to be heard over the crackle of flames. "The fire's too strong!"

"Corben's in there!" snapped Longarm. "I've got to get him out." The outlaw still represented his best hope of discovering the truth in the murder of Jericho Malone.

Davis caught at Longarm's sleeve. "You can't go in there!" he said. "Wait'll the bucket brigade gets here! They ought to be on the way!"

It was true that many of Harkerville's citizens were running toward the jail, eager to help contain the blaze and find out what had happened. But by the time they got the fire put out, it would be too late. Longarm was sure of that. Corben would be dead—if he wasn't already.

Longarm shook off Davis's hand, pulled his hat down

tightly, and ran toward the blasted-out opening in the rear wall of the jail. The heat from the blaze beat at him as he came closer. He flinched back for a second but didn't stop. He ducked his head and hurdled into the jail, leaping over a burning beam.

The smoke was so thick that he couldn't see much, but from the debris he kept tripping over, he figured this had been the center of the explosion. The smoke made him cough and stung his eyes. He pulled off his bandanna and held it over his nose and mouth to try to filter out some of the acrid haze. "Corben!" he yelled, and his voice sounded strange to his ears. "Corben, you in here?"

Nothing but the crackle of the flames came to his ears. The stone outer walls and floor of the jail wouldn't burn, but the roof and the inner walls and the furnishings were all ablaze. Longarm stumbled on something again and this time fell to his knees.

He put a hand down to catch himself and felt it encounter something soft and wet. He heard a faint moan. "Corben!" Longarm called. "Corben, is that you?"

A louder groan sounded. Longarm tied the bandanna around his face, then used both hands to explore the shape on which he had landed. It was vaguely human, and that was enough for him. He got his arms around it and staggered to his feet.

Now he had to get out of this inferno, which wasn't going to be easy because he wasn't quite sure where the opening was in the wall. He was so turned around and blinded by the smoke, in fact, that he didn't even know in which direction the rear of the jail lay.

Turning slowly with his grisly burden clutched to him, he tried to judge which way the heat was the strongest and then headed away from it. After a second he could tell that the smoke was billowing in the same direction, which meant he was going the right way. As coughs wracked his body, he stumbled out through the hole left by the blast. The smoke thinned, and he gratefully sucked down some air that was at least a little cleaner and fresher.

Hands reached out, grabbed him, guided him away from the blaze. The limp weight in his arms went away. Through the tears that still filled his eyes, Longarm began to see the anxious face of Sheriff Harold Davis. "Over here!" Davis shouted at him. "You're safe now, Marshal!"

Longarm had other worries besides his own safety. "Corben!" he rasped. "Where's Corben?"

"You got him out of there," Davis assured him.

With Davis's hand firmly gripping his arm, Longarm moved away from the burning jail. He found himself sitting under a tree with his back against the trunk, bracing himself as more hard coughs shook him. He took off his hat and wiped a hand across his face. It came away covered with soot. He probably looked like he belonged in a minstrel show, thought Longarm. "Just call me Mister Bones," he muttered under his breath.

Davis knelt beside him. "What was that?" the sheriff asked.

Longarm waved away the question. "Where's Corben?" His vision was clearing now, and he could see the crowd of townspeople in the alley. A bucket brigade had formed, just as Davis had said it would, and the citizens of Harkerville were throwing buckets of water onto the conflagration. Their efforts would be too little, too late, however, Longarm knew. Nothing could save the jail and sheriff's office now, but at least the fire wouldn't spread to the rest of the settlement.

"Corben's right here," Davis said. He nodded to the side.

The grim tone of the sheriff's voice told Longarm almost all he needed to know. He looked over and saw the heap of blistered, smoking flesh beside him. Corben must have been close to the blast when it occurred. His clothes had been blown and burned off him, and his body had a funny shape to it, as if a giant fist had pounded him into something that was barely recognizable as human. Longarm didn't see how anything that looked like that could still be alive.

But Corben was.

A groan came from the grotesque thing. Longarm leaned over it and said urgently, "Corben! Corben, can you hear me? What happened?"

With a flicker of eyelids from which the lashes had been scorched off, Corben opened his eyes and looked up at Longarm. For a second, Corben didn't seem to see anything, then his tormented gaze settled on the face of the big lawman.

"Didn't . . . didn't think they'd really . . . do it," came a strangled croak.

Longarm made a guess. "Your pards from the gang who got away, they tossed some sticks of dynamite into your cell, didn't they?"

"We all . . . knew . . . Walt told us . . . don't get caught . . . had to . . . cover the trail . . ."

Longarm's pulse, already pounding from the effort of getting Corben out of the burning jail, now sped up even more. The survivors from the gang, instead of trying to rescue Corben from custody, had come to Harkerville to kill him instead. The only reason they'd do that was to make sure Corben wouldn't talk. And if they would go to such lengths to insure his silence, that had to mean that he knew something worth telling.

"What about it, Corben?" Longarm insisted. "Did you think of something that'll tell me what I need to know? Who gave the orders to Springer?"

"Don't know . . . All Walt ever said . . . was rainbow . . . man . . ."

Rainbow man? thought Longarm. What the hell . . . ?

Corben gasped, and his back arched. He threw his head back. His lips formed a bloodless line across his ruined face as they drew tightly together. Then, with what sounded almost like a sigh of relief, the outlaw relaxed, and his head fell slowly to the side. His eyes were still open, but they weren't seeing anything.

Sheriff Davis put a hand on Longarm's shoulder.

"Reckon he's gone," the sheriff said. "What was that he said, right there at the last?"

"Rainbow man," repeated Longarm.

"What in blazes does that mean?"

Longarm looked up, met Davis's puzzled gaze, and shook his head. "I wish I knew."

Chapter 19

It was Sunday evening when Longarm got back to Denver. He dropped off the horse at the livery stable and then went to the boardinghouse where he had his rented room. He would have stopped at a barbershop for a bath and a shave, but they were all closed. Instead he had to haul in the metal tub from the storage shed out back, heat his own water, and dump it in the tub himself. It was an inconvenience, but he didn't want to go see Janice Parmalee until he had cleaned up some from his trip to the mountains.

His hands and face still tingled a little from the minor burns he had received while he was getting Johnny Corben out of the Harkerville jail. He had rubbed bear grease on the burns, said grease being provided by Sheriff Davis, but that was about all he could do other than wait for them to heal.

Naturally, Davis had been mighty upset about the destruction of his office and jail. He didn't live there, however, so it wasn't like he had lost everything. After the fire was put out, the stone walls of the building were still standing, and the townspeople had promised to rebuild the interior and put a new roof on it. That would take a few weeks, but then things would get back to normal in Harkerville.

Longarm wished he could say the same about his own life. He was convinced of Estelle Malone's innocence, convinced as well that his testimony might help to convict her despite her innocence. But although he was sure he had figured out who was really behind Jericho Malone's death, he had no way of proving it.

All during the long ride back, he had turned over the facts of the case in his mind, trying to remember something he had overlooked. There was nothing. Nor had he thought of anything that would tell him what Corben had meant by Rainbow Man. If Longarm had heard the dying outlaw correctly, that was what Walt Springer had called the man who gave Springer his orders and the inside information about the silver shipments. That had to be Howard Summerlin. If only Longarm had any evidence . . .

Once he had the bath ready, he took off his clothes and sank down gratefully into the hot water. As the heat soaked into his stiff, sore muscles and relaxed them, a sense of drowsiness stole over Longarm. He tried to fight it, but he was simply too tired. He dozed off.

When he awoke, he wasn't sure how long he had been asleep. He stood up, dripping, and reached for his watch, which he had left on a chair close to the tub along with his gun, his cheroots, and a packet of lucifers. Almost nine o'clock, he saw as he opened the watch. That was late, but maybe not too late. No matter what the hour, he wanted to see Janice Parmalee so that he could fill her in on what he had learned on his trip, as well as finding out from her what had happened in court on the previous Friday.

He dried off and pulled on socks, underwear, and trousers, then took out his razor and scraped the beard stubble off his face. After slapping on some bay rum, he finished dressing, then paused to take a swig from the bottle of Maryland rye that sat on the table beside his bed. He felt at least partially human again as he left the boardinghouse and set out for the hotel in downtown Denver where Janice was staying.

When he knocked on the door of her room, she called immediately, "Just a moment, please." The promptness of her answer told him that he hadn't roused her from sleep, and he was glad of that. He heard light footsteps on the other side of the door, then Janice asked, "Who is it?"

"Marshal Long."

The key rattled in the lock, and Janice opened the door. She smiled at him and said, "Come in, Marshal."

She wore the same silk dressing gown she had worn on Longarm's previous late evening visit to her room. Her hair was loose around her shoulders and her face was free of cosmetics. She looked younger than he knew she really was.

Janice closed the door behind Longarm. "I've been hoping to see you," she said. "I knew you planned to be back in Denver today if possible. Did you find out anything in your visit to Mr. Malone's mine?"

"Maybe," Longarm said. He took off his hat.

Janice stepped forward quickly and said, "Let me take that for you." That brought her close enough to him so that he could smell a faint hint of perfume coming from her. Or maybe that was just her natural scent, he thought. Either way, it was sweet and intriguing.

She took his hat and set it on the dresser, then turned back to him and asked, "Can I get you something to drink? I have some brandy that my father brought with him. For medicinal purposes, of course."

"Of course," Longarm agreed. "But no, I reckon I'm just fine."

"All right." She came closer to him again. "Tell me what you found."

"A possible motive for Howard Summerlin to have killed his boss and framed Mrs. Malone for the killing," Longarm said.

Excitement flared in Janice's eyes, only to be tempered

a second later. "A *possible* motive, you said. You're not sure?"

Longarm had expected her to catch that. He said, "I've got a theory, but no evidence to back it up."

Janice took a deep breath and nodded. "Tell me," she said.

Longarm did so, starting with Sheriff Harold Davis's first mention of the holdups plaguing the silver shipments from the Colorado Star mine. He told Janice about his visit to the mine and his meeting with Ben Jeppson, the foreman. "From the sound of it, somebody who knows about the shipments ahead of time has been tipping off the gang."

Janice's quick mind leaped ahead. "Summerlin," she said. "And when Jericho Malone found out about it, Summerlin killed him and then placed the blame on Mrs. Malone."

Longarm nodded. "It sounds right to me. And it ties up even neater than that once you consider what one of the outlaws told me."

"One of the outlaws?" Janice repeated. "You talked to one of the outlaws?"

Longarm told her about the attempted robbery he had broken up and his capture of the owlhoot named Johnny Corben. "Corben told me that the fella who was ramrodding the gang got his orders from somebody else. Whoever it was told them which shipments to hit."

Janice began to pace back and forth. "It has to be Summerlin," she declared. "That's the only answer that makes any sense."

"Yeah. I hoped to get some solid proof out of Corben, but his friends came to see him in jail before I could do that."

"What do you mean? Did they help him escape?"

"They killed him to keep him from talking," Longarm said. "Tossed a bundle of dynamite into the cell where he was locked up."

Janice's right hand went to her mouth. "Oh, my God. How horrible."

"It sure was," Longarm agreed. "I got to Corben before he died and tried to talk to him, but he only said one thing, and it's got me plumb mystified."

"What did he say?"

"Rainbow Man."

Janice frowned. "But that doesn't make any sense."

"Nope. It doesn't. And it sure doesn't point to Summerlin, even though I'm convinced he's guilty."

"After what you've told me, I am, too." Janice looked around the room. "My goodness, I've kept you standing all this time. Please, Marshal, sit down."

Longarm took the single chair while Janice sat on the edge of the bed. He thought she looked mighty nice perched there. The robe she wore hiked up a little as she sat, so that her bare ankles and the bottom part of her calves were revealed. She wore a pair of soft slippers on her feet.

"I reckon that's all I've got to tell you," Longarm said. "What happened in court Friday?"

"I called a procession of character witnesses, as I said I would. Mr. Creighton didn't like it, but he couldn't find anything to object to that the judge would sustain. I'm afraid Judge Walton got rather impatient, too, however, so I'm glad you're back. I think he would have shut down that line of testimony tomorrow if I'd tried to persist in it."

"Did the witnesses help Mrs. Malone any?"

"I doubt it. Mr. Creighton tried to shake them and get them to admit to something dreadful that Mrs. Malone might have done in the past, but there wasn't anything. Still, character witnesses can only help a defendant so much when the facts of the case are seemingly against her, as they are here."

"What are you going to do tomorrow?"

Janice frowned in thought for a moment, then said, "I

think we have to introduce the matter of the silver robberies."

"There's no evidence tying Summerlin to them," Longarm pointed out.

"No, but they'll muddy the waters and show that Mr. Malone had other troubles besides those caused by his wife. We're just trying to establish reasonable doubt, Marshal."

"Seems like the best way to do that would be to prove who really killed Malone," Longarm said with a frown.

"Yes, of course, but failing that, we have to convince the jury that someone else besides Mrs. Malone was just as likely to have committed the crime, even if we can't prove who that someone is."

Longarm shook his head. "Seems shaky to me."

"It is, but what else can we do?"

"That's the problem, all right." He rubbed his jaw. "The barrel of a gun against his head might get Summerlin to tell the truth."

"A forced confession is worthless."

"Not when it's true."

"I won't argue the law with you, Marshal. All I can say is that Judge Walton has made it plain he wants everything done properly. He's holding everything to the most stringent standard. This may be the West, but such wild and woolly methods simply won't work in this case."

"Damned shame, too," Longarm muttered. He came to his feet.

Janice stood up, as well, and stepped over to him so that she could put a hand on his arm. "I understand your frustration, Marshal. We both wanted you to find something that would positively clear Mrs. Malone. But without that, all we can do is proceed as best we can."

"I reckon you're right." Longarm looked down into her face. "How's your father doing?"

"His recovery is progressing nicely, the doctor says. In another few weeks, he should be able to travel and we can return to New York."

The trial would be over by then, one way or the other, Longarm knew. But he suddenly found that the idea of Janice Parmalee leaving Denver didn't sit well with him.

"I reckon you'll be glad to get home," he said.

"Of course. But I have to admit . . . there are some things I'll miss about Denver."

She was looking up at him as she said it, and somehow she had gotten closer to him, so that their bodies were almost touching. Those hazel eyes of hers were so big and soft Longarm felt as if he were about to tumble right into them. He felt the warmth of her breath on his neck.

He thought about it for a second, then mentally told himself the hell with it. He raised his hand, put a finger under her chin, and tilted her head back. Her eyes closed, and he brought his mouth down on hers.

For a moment, they were only touching in those two places—their lips, and his finger under her chin. But as the kiss grew more urgent, she leaned into him so that he felt the soft, yet insistent pressure of her slender body all up and down his muscular form. His left arm went around her waist and pressed her more tightly to him. His tongue explored her lips. They parted, inviting him into the warm, wet cavern of her mouth. As his tongue thrust forward, her tongue met it, darting out to fence sensuously with the invader.

As he kissed her, the fingertips of Longarm's right hand left her chin and trailed down her throat. He moved the lapel of the dressing gown aside and slipped his hand underneath it. He knew from the feel of her body in his embrace that she was wearing little or nothing under the silken robe. As his palm slid over the modest rise of her breast, he confirmed that she was nude under the silk. The erect nipple that crowned her left breast prodded against his palm.

Janice moaned as he captured that nipple between thumb and forefinger and pulled gently on it. Her hips lifted and came forward, molding her pelvis against his groin. Longarm's shaft was stiffening, rising inexorably to the tempting pressure.

Longarm broke the kiss, unwilling to take advantage of her. He said, "If you ain't sure this is a good idea—"

"I think it's a very good idea indeed," Janice said. Her arms went around his neck and pulled his head down to hers again.

Well, he told himself, if this was what she wanted, he was more than willing to oblige. His manhood was as long and hard as an iron bar by now, and if the way Janice was grinding her belly against it was any indication, she was as anxious as he was to get it inside her.

Longarm found the belt of the robe where it was tied around Janice's waist and loosened the knot. As the belt fell away, he spread the robe apart, peeled it back off her shoulders, and let it fall loosely to the floor around her feet. She was completely nude now except for the slippers. He bent down and tongued first one hard nipple and then the other. She took hold of his hand and brought it between her thighs. He felt the fine hair that grew there, then found the hot, slick dampness that was waiting for him. His middle finger slipped into her, probing her female core.

"Oh!" Janice gasped. "Marshal!"

"Call me Custis," said Longarm. He thought a little more familiarity was appropriate, considering where he had his finger right now.

"Oh, Custis . . . what you're doing to me . . ."

"Want me to stop?" Longarm asked.

"No!" Her fingers bit hard into his shoulders. "Please, no."

They were only a few steps from the bed. Longarm gradually worked Janice toward it until the back of her knees hit the edge of the mattress. She let herself go then, tumbling backward onto the comforter. She lay with her chest heaving from passion and her legs parted so that Longarm had a good view of the fleshy folds he had just been fondling.

"Please get undressed and make love to me," Janice whispered. "I need you so much, Custis."

Longarm shed his duds as fast as he could, and when he pulled down his long underwear and allowed his shaft to spring free, Janice sat up with a small cry of wonderment. "I never dreamed . . . ," she said. "How will we ever fit all of that inside me?" She reached up to wrap both hands around his shaft.

"I reckon we'll find a way," Longarm said as he enjoyed the way Janice stroked his organ with that two-handed grip. He still wasn't sure if she was a virgin or not. The way she was staring at him and playing with him, she was acting like she'd never seen such a thing before.

She looked up at him shyly. "Can I . . . kiss it?"

He stroked her hair and said, "Careful-like. You don't want to get all messed up."

"I'm not sure I'd mind . . . as long as it's you doing the messing, Custis."

With that, she leaned forward and pressed her lips to the head of his shaft, right at the opening. She moved around it, nuzzling the entire crown, then kissed down its length.

"How can it be so hard and so soft at the same time? It's like kissing velvet, yet it has such an aura of power."

Longarm closed his eyes. Leave it to a lawyer to start talking, he thought.

But then Janice didn't say anything else for a while, because she opened her mouth and took him inside, making urgent little sucking sounds as she swallowed more and more of the fleshy pole.

Longarm rested both hands on her head as she sucked him. She was a little awkward at it, scraping her teeth on him a time or two, convincing him that she hadn't done *this* before, no matter what else she might have done. But she had a natural talent for speaking French, and within minutes he felt his climax edging closer. Not wanting to spend in her mouth, he moved his hands to her shoulders and pressed her back onto the mattress. Her mouth remained open, the lips slack with desire.

He thought about giving her the same sort of oral pleasure she had just given him, but then decided that neither of them could stand the delay. Moving over her, he poised himself between her widespread thighs and brought the head of his shaft to her opening. Her sex was drenched and ready. Longarm thrust forward with his hips, sliding into her.

Janice's arms went around him, clutching at him with surprising strength as he filled her. Her sheath clasped hotly around his organ. She drew her knees up and pumped her hips, meeting his thrusts with her own as he launched into a timeless rhythm.

Her breasts were crushed against his chest. He kissed her again, drinking in the hot sweetness of her mouth. He plunged his manhood in and out of her half a dozen times, and that was all it took to topple her over the edge. She screamed into his mouth as her hips jerked wildly in the grip of her climax. Longarm felt the flood of female dew around his shaft.

He intended to hold back, so that he could prolong the enjoyment for her, but he couldn't fight the sensations that washed over him. While she was still quivering with her own culmination, he drove as deep inside her as he could reach and began to spasm. Hot, thick cream shot up his shaft and burst out in spurt after scalding spurt. He held himself there, deep within, and let his seed erupt, filling her.

After what seemed like hours, the shuddering finally stopped. Longarm had kept enough presence of mind to support his weight on his knees and elbows so that he wouldn't crush her, but just barely. He slid out of her and sprawled on his back next to her, his chest heaving as he tried to catch his breath. Beside him, Janice was equally breathless.

"My . . . my goodness," Janice was finally able to say.

"Custis, that . . . that was . . . I just can't find the words!"

Which just went to show you, thought Longarm, that under the right circumstances, even a lawyer could be struck speechless.

Chapter 20

Janice looked all prim and proper as she came into the courtroom the next morning, Longarm thought as he watched her from his seat in the spectators' section. Just judging by her appearance, nobody would guess she had spent half the night indulging herself in the pleasures of the flesh with a deputy United States marshal. And damned enthusiastically, too. After she'd had his manhood inside her once, she seemed determined to prove that she could take it again in every possible opening in her body.

After thinking about that for a few minutes, Longarm cleared his throat and shifted his Stetson on his lap to hide the erection that had popped up. He gave himself a stern mental warning to get his thoughts back on the case.

Janice didn't seem to have anything else on her mind this morning. She didn't even glace in Longarm's direction as she sat down at the defense table and took several papers from her portfolio. A few moments later, the guards brought in Estelle Malone, who took her usual seat next to Janice. The two women spoke together in low tones.

Longarm and Janice hadn't spent *all* their time together romping in bed. Part of the night, they had discussed the case, going around and around in the same circles and finally reaching the same conclusions. As unsatisfactory as it was, Janice had no choice now except to introduce the matter of the silver robberies, in an attempt to create doubt in the minds of the jury as to Estelle Malone's guilt. That meant she would have to call Longarm as a witness.

More spectators were filing into the courtroom. Longarm turned his head to watch them and saw Howard Summerlin taking a seat next to Natalie Malone. Longarm's eyes narrowed as he gazed at Summerlin. He was looking at Malone's murderer, he knew, but that knowledge wasn't going to do anyone any good.

To have set up those robberies, Summerlin had to be a greedy son of a bitch, thought Longarm. Maybe he had come up with the scheme on his own, or maybe he had been prompted by Belle Cardwell. Either way, Summerlin was out to make a fortune in stolen silver, and he wasn't going to let anything stand in his way.

Suddenly, Longarm stiffened in his chair. One of the answers to his dilemma had been staring him in the face all along, he realized with an unexpected flash of insight. But in order to take advantage of it, he had to talk to Janice before the trial resumed. He stood up and moved over behind the defense table, then leaned toward her and called her name. Janice turned around, looking startled.

"I have to talk to you," Longarm said.

"But the judge will be coming out of his chambers any minute—"

"Then we better make it quick," urged Longarm.

Janice nodded and came to her feet. "All right." She patted Estelle's shoulder. "I'll be right back."

Together, they stepped from the courtroom into the hall. As they left the courtroom, Longarm felt Summerlin watching them. He regretted that, but it couldn't be helped.

"What is it, Marshal?" Janice asked briskly, all business now.

"I hate to say it, but you got to stall some more. I can't

testify today, and you can't bring up those robberies."

"But why not?" Janice exclaimed. "That's all we have left."

Longarm shook his head. "Maybe not. I need another couple of days, Janice. Can you give them to me?"

She searched his face intently for a moment, then sighed and nodded. "I can try. I can't guarantee anything, though. The judge may shut me off."

Longarm put a hand on her shoulder and squeezed. "Do the best you can. And when we go back in there, look mad at me."

"What?"

"I want you to look at me like I did or said something to really rile you up."

"I don't understand any of this," Janice said. "But I trust you, Custis."

When they reentered the courtroom, Janice was glaring at him as if she would have gladly bitten his head off. Longarm returned the hostile stare as Janice returned to the defense table. Instead of resuming his seat, he moved along the rows of benches until he was behind the one where Summerlin and Natalie Malone were sitting. Summerlin looked surprised as Longarm put a hand on his shoulder and bent over to speak quietly into his ear.

"Something's come up you need to know about, Mr. Summerlin," Longarm said.

Summerlin looked up at him. "What is it?"

"Come out into the hall with me."

Summerlin hesitated, then said to Natalie, "I'll be right back, my dear." He stood up and followed Longarm out of the courtroom into the corridor.

"What's all this about, Marshal?" Summerlin demanded when he and Longarm were standing by themselves, a few feet from the door of the courtroom.

"I know you and me ain't been too friendly so far in this case," Longarm said, "but you're lookin' out for the Malone business holdings, aren't you?"

"That's right."

"Well, I been out to the Colorado Star mine the past few days."

Summerlin looked genuinely surprised. "You have?"

Longarm nodded. "I found out that an outlaw gang has been holding up some of the shipments between the mine and the town of Harkerville, where the nearest rail line is."

"Yes, yes, I know all about that. I'm in fairly close contact with Ben Jeppson, the mine superintendent."

"But you didn't know that I busted up the last holdup attempt, did you?"

"What?" Summerlin looked more than surprised now. He seemed shocked.

"A couple of days ago," said Longarm, "those owlhoots who have been hitting the silver wagons tried again, but I was waiting for them. I broke up the robbery, killed a few of the bandits, and ran off the others."

Summerlin took a handkerchief from his pocket and wiped his forehead. "Were . . . were you able to capture any of the desperadoes?"

Regretfully, Longarm shook his head. "Nope." This was the first outright lie he had told to Summerlin. He was convinced, however, that Summerlin wouldn't know the difference. No one except the dead gang leader, Walt Springer, had known who the real boss of the outfit was. The surviving gang members had followed the orders Springer had given them to make sure that no prisoners were allowed to talk, but that was as far as they could carry it. They had no way to pass along any information to Summerlin, because they didn't know who he was.

Summerlin shrugged and put away his handkerchief. "That's a shame. If you'd been able to catch one of them, he might have put you on the trail of the others. All I can do is thank you, Marshal, for saving that shipment for the estate."

"Well, I didn't actually save anything," Longarm said.

Summerlin frowned. "What do you mean?"

"That shipment was a decoy. Jeppson didn't really send any silver."

Now he was taking a risk. He didn't know if the silver shipped from Harkerville had arrived in Denver yet or not. If it had, there was a good chance Summerlin already knew about it. If not, Longarm had a chance to lay a trap for the man.

Right away, he knew he'd been lucky. Summerlin sputtered, "What? Jeppson didn't send the silver?"

"Nope." Longarm lowered his voice and went on confidentially, "It's going out from the mine tomorrow morning. Now that I've busted up the gang, there's no more danger of a holdup."

"Well, thank God for that," Summerlin said fervently. "But why are you telling me this, Marshal?" A trace of suspicion lingered in his eyes. "I saw you talking to that Parmalee woman a few minutes ago."

Longarm waved a hand. "She's got some crazy idea in her head that those robberies have something to do with Malone's murder. I was telling her not to bother calling me as a witness, because there was nothing I could say that would help her."

"She could force you to testify with a subpoena," Summerlin pointed out.

"Not if I ain't in town," Longarm said with a grin.

"Where are you going?"

"My boss, Billy Vail, has a job for me to handle up in Montana. He said I've been hangin' around this courthouse wastin' the taxpayers' money long enough." Longarm took out his watch and opened it. "Fact is, I've got to catch a train in less than an hour. I just wanted you to know you don't have to worry about those silver holdups anymore."

Summerlin nodded solemnly. "I appreciate that consideration, Marshal. By the time you get back, the trial will surely be over."

"I hope so," Longarm said, trying to sound as sincere as possible. "I'm ready to see justice done."

"I thought you believed in Mrs. Malone's innocence," said Summerlin, frowning slightly again.

"I never said that. I just didn't want to see her railroaded. If anything was going to come up to clear her name, though, I reckon it would have by now."

"But it hasn't, because she *is* guilty."

"Sure looks that way," Longarm agreed. He put out his right hand. "So long, Mr. Summerlin."

"Have a good trip to Montana, Marshal," Summerlin replied as he shook Longarm's hand.

Longarm waited until he was out of the courthouse before he wiped his hand against his trousers.

Summerlin had taken the bait, all right. It remained to be seen what he would do with it. In the meantime, Longarm had a lot of details to tend to. He had to talk to Billy Vail and make sure Vail would back up his story if necessary. Once Longarm laid out the whole thing, he felt sure Vail would cooperate. Even more urgent, he had to get a wire off to Ben Jeppson, in care of Sheriff Davis, and he had to find out the whereabouts of that load of silver taken to Harkerville a couple of days earlier. With Jeppson and Davis backing his play, he thought he could have that silver stashed someplace where Summerlin couldn't find it. The whole plan rested on that.

Actually, it was all a gamble, thought Longarm as he hurried away from the courthouse, just like the roll of the dice or the turn of a card.

Only in this game, the payoff was liable to be in hot lead.

Chapter 21

The three wagons were loaded in the predawn darkness, but they didn't leave the Colorado Star mine until nearly an hour after sunrise. Only four men accompanied the convoy this time—a driver on each wagon, plus one rider who moseyed along the trail in front of the vehicles.

Longarm rode in the lead wagon, stretched out on his back in the wagon bed, his hat wadded up under his head to serve as a crude pillow. His head pointed toward the front of the wagon, his feet toward the rear. In the stuffy air under the canvas shroud, he could smell the oil from the Winchester that lay across his chest.

Stacks of silver ingots rose around him, forming a cave of sorts. The canvas was stretched tight and tied in place so that it wouldn't sag in the middle and reveal the hollow space where Longarm was concealed. The loads in the other wagons were hollowed out in similar fashion, and each of them had a surprise waiting inside, too, in the form of deputies from Denver who had ridden out here to the Colorado Star with Longarm. In addition, Sheriff Harold Davis was waiting with a posse high in the mountains above the route the wagons would take to Harkerville. Davis and the other men had ridden into the mountains by a roundabout course and had made a cold camp the night before so they wouldn't be spotted by anybody keeping an eye on the trail.

As the wagon rocked along, Longarm thought that he had done just about all he could do. All of his preparations might come to nothing. There was no way of knowing. But he had to make the attempt.

The convoy wound its way through the mountains toward Harkerville. Covered up and in the dark like he was, Longarm had no way of knowing how much ground they had covered since leaving the mine. It seemed like a lot of time had passed and that they ought to be getting to the settlement, but he told himself that was just his brain playing tricks on him. He felt himself getting drowsy. This wasn't the most comfortable place he had ever been, but the past twenty-four hours had been busy ones. He tried not to doze off.

The sudden crack of a gunshot cutting through the clear mountain air made certain that he didn't fall asleep. His eyes opened wide and his hands tightened on the Winchester. The wagon drivers had their orders: At the first sign of trouble, they were to stop the wagons and put up their hands as if they were surrendering.

More shots sounded as the wagon in which Longarm was riding jolted to a halt. His teeth ground together in frustration. He had to wait for the trap to spring shut properly, but after all this time, waiting was difficult. He wanted to get this over with.

After a couple of tense moments, Longarm heard hoofbeats approaching the wagons. A harsh, muffled voice called out, "Just keep them hands elevated, boys, and we won't have to ventilate you!"

The driver on the lead wagon, an old miner named Everett, said, "What is it you skunks want?"

The same gravelly voice that had spoken before replied, "What do you think we want, old-timer? We want that silver you're haulin'!"

That was enough for Longarm. He rolled over, jerked the slipknot that freed one corner of the canvas cover, and came up on his knees. He surged to his feet, throwing aside the canvas as he did so. "How about some lead instead?" he bellowed as he brought up the Winchester.

His eyes, accustomed to the gloom under the canvas, had to adjust quickly to the morning sunlight as guns began to boom. The voice of the outlaw who had spoken gave him his first target. He fired three shots as fast as he could work the rifle's lever, spraying the bullets toward the side of the trail. He saw several men on horseback bunched there, and one of them went flying backward out of the saddle as the slugs from Longarm's Winchester punched into his chest.

Back on the other two wagons, the hidden deputies had heard Longarm's shout and were now throwing off their own concealment to join the fracas. The drivers and the single guard, who had all been waiting with their hands up, slapped leather as well. In a heartbeat, the battle was on.

Longarm pivoted, his eyes searching the holdup men for the familiar figure he hoped would be there. Sure enough, hanging back from the others was a smaller rider, and like a flash, another of Longarm's questions was answered. Like the rest of the outlaws, the man had a bandanna tied over the lower half of his face to mask his features. This man's bandanna, instead of the red check or solid color of the others, was a bright mixture of all the colors in the rainbow.

There were half a dozen bandits, not counting the man in the rainbow-colored bandanna. Longarm had already downed one of them, and another was doubled over in his saddle, blood welling over the fingers he pressed to his midsection. Longarm rattled off three more shots and saw one of the outlaws clutch a bullet-shattered shoulder. Lead sang past Longarm's ear as he drew a bead and fired again. This time the bullet thudded into the center of an outlaw's forehead and burst out the back of his skull. At the same moment, yet another outlaw went spinning to the ground from the back of his madly dancing horse as a shot from one of the other deputies found him.

That was enough. The other holdup men cut and run, spinning their horses around and throwing the spurs to the animals. The man in the rainbow-colored bandanna was more awkward than the others and had trouble controlling his mount, but he managed to get it started in a gallop back along the trail, taking a different direction than the rest of the outlaws.

Longarm didn't care about the others. He figured they were either survivors from the original gang or new members hastily recruited for this job. They would be rounded up by Sheriff Davis's posse. But Longarm wanted the Rainbow Man.

He set his rifle aside and waved over the guard on horseback. "Give me your horse," he called as he stepped up to the driver's box of the wagon.

The guard swung down hurriedly from the horse, and without even climbing down to the ground first, Longarm leaped from the wagon into the saddle. He grabbed the reins, his feet found the stirrups, and he dug the heels of his boots into the horse's flanks. The horse lunged ahead.

Longarm leaned forward in the saddle as his borrowed mount raced after the quarry. The animal's hooves pounded a tattoo on the trail. Longarm was a much more skillful rider than the man he was chasing. He began to close the gap almost right away. By the time he had covered a quarter of a mile, he was drawing within pistol range of the fleeing bandit.

Longarm didn't want to shoot the man out of the saddle, though. He had to be taken alive. That was the only thing that would end this.

Gradually, Longarm drew closer and closer. His horse was running well, and he knew it was only a matter of time before he caught up to the other man. The man turned his head to throw a frantic glance over his shoulder, and Longarm saw that the brightly colored bandanna mask had slipped down, revealing the pale, terrified face of Howard Summerlin. Longarm felt a surge of satisfaction that he had been right all along.

By now, Longarm's mount was galloping along less than ten feet behind Summerlin's. Longarm urged a little more speed out of the horse, and as it stretched out into a longer gait, its nose drew even with the other horse's hindquarters.

Suddenly, Summerlin twisted in the saddle, and Longarm saw the glint of sunlight reflecting off steel. He ducked low over his horse's neck as the gun in Summerlin's hand exploded. Longarm knew he wasn't hit, and his horse never broke stride, so he knew the shot had missed. He didn't give Summerlin time to try another.

As his mount surged up even with Summerlin's, Longarm left the saddle in a lunging dive that carried him into the other man. Summerlin cried out as the impact of Longarm's body drove him sideways. Longarm wrapped his arms tightly around Summerlin as both of them fell.

They slammed into the ground, and the crash knocked them apart. Longarm's momentum carried him on. He rolled over a couple of times. When he stopped, he came up on his hands and knees and saw a dazed Howard Summerlin trying to get up. Summerlin shook his head, then lunged toward the gun he had dropped when Longarm tackled him. The revolver was lying on the ground several feet away from where the two men had landed.

Longarm didn't give Summerlin time to reach the weapon. He threw himself forward, crashing into the smaller man again. Summerlin rolled over and lashed out at Longarm with his fists. He was no rough-and-tumble brawler, but desperation lent him strength and speed that he didn't normally possess. He landed a punch on Longarm's jaw that stopped the big lawman—but only for a second.

Then Longarm's fist smashed into Summerlin's face and drove the man's head back against the ground. Longarm reared up on his knees and threw another punch.

Summerlin's head rocked to the side under the impact. He was limp now, only half-conscious.

Longarm came to his feet, reached down, and balled his fist in the shirt and vest Summerlin was wearing. He straightened, hauling Summerlin to his feet.

"D-Don't hit me again," Summerlin muttered. "Wh-What're you going to do with me?"

"I reckon you know that as well as I do, old son," Longarm said as he stepped back and drew his gun so that he could cover Summerlin. "You and me got an appointment in court."

". . . running out of patience, Counselor," Judge Walton was saying angrily as Longarm stepped into the Denver courtroom late that afternoon. He had ridden hard in order to get here in time, before the trial of Estelle Malone was adjourned for the day. He could have waited until the next morning, he supposed, but he was anxious to bring this farce to a close.

Janice was on her feet in front of the judge's bench. "I'm sorry, Your Honor," she said. "I was simply trying to establish a pattern of behavior—"

"A pattern to which the prosecution has already stipulated, as it has no material bearing on the case at hand," Abercrombie Creighton said from his table.

"I have to agree with Mr. Creighton," Judge Walton said. "You've wasted three days of the court's time, Miss Parmalee, and I refuse to allow you to waste any more of it. Call your next witness, and they'd better have something material to offer."

"Your Honor, since it's late in the day, an adjournment might be in order—"

"I'll decide what's in order!" Walton cut in, interrupting Janice. "Either call a witness or rest your case, Counselor."

Janice glanced around, and Longarm saw the hopelessness on her face. Then her eyes spotted him standing at the back of the courtroom in his dusty range clothes. He nodded to her and poked himself in the chest with a thumb as he used his other hand to take off his hat.

Janice turned back toward the bench. "Your Honor, I call Deputy Marshal Custis Long."

Creighton jumped to his feet for that one. "Objection, Your Honor! Marshal Long has already testified as a witness for the prosecution!"

"Which in no way prevents him from testifying for the defense as well," Janice said. Her voice was firmer now. Clearly, she had drawn some strength from Longarm's presence in the courtroom.

Judge Walton leaned forward. "Let me get this straight, Miss Parmalee. You're not re-calling Marshal Long for further cross-examination?"

"No, Your Honor."

"Are you calling him as a hostile witness?"

Janice glanced at Longarm, and he slowly shook his head. She said, "No, Your Honor."

Walton sat back. He cocked his head to the side and said, "This should be good." With a wave of his hand, he instructed, "Call your witness, Counselor."

"Deputy Marshal Custis Long," Janice said again.

Longarm came forward through the gate in the railing and dropped his hat on the defense table. He smiled down at Estelle Malone, who peered up at him in confusion and anxiety. Then he went to the witness stand, where he was sworn in and took his seat.

Before Janice could begin asking questions, Walton wrinkled his nose and said, "You smell of horse, Marshal."

"I'd be surprised if I didn't, Your Honor," Longarm said. "I been on one almost all day."

"Very well. Proceed, Miss Parmalee."

Janice stepped closer to the witness stand, and her eyes searched Longarm's. She had no real idea what he was going to say, he realized. It would have been nice if they'd had a few minutes to go over his testimony, but they hadn't been afforded that luxury. She would just have to follow his lead.

"Marshal, you've already testified in this case," Janice said. "Are we to understand that you now have more information to give us?"

"Yes, ma'am, that's right," Longarm said.

"Why don't you . . . go ahead and do that."

She was giving him free rein. Longarm said, "Yes, ma'am. A few days ago, I sat here and told the court about what I'd seen and heard on the night of Jericho Malone's death. I know now there was more to the story than that. Jericho Malone owned a silver mine called the Colorado Star—"

Creighton said, "Objection, Your Honor. Mr. Malone's ownership of the Colorado Star mine is a matter of record. It hardly qualifies as new information."

"Well, the fact that owlhoots have been holding up his silver shipments for the past six months ain't in the record," snapped Longarm. He looked over at Walton. "Sorry, Your Honor."

"That's all right, Marshal. I know from conversations with Chief Marshal Vail that decorum is not your strong suit, shall we say. The objection is overruled."

Janice said, "These silver robberies, do they have a connection with Mr. Malone's death?"

"Sure they do," said Longarm. "They caused it. Somebody was tipping off the gang every time a big shipment was going out, and Malone found out who was doing it. So that fella had to kill him."

"Objection!" Creighton roared. "This is sheer speculation! The witness is doing nothing more than . . . than spinning a yarn!"

Walton asked, "Do you have any proof of your statement, Marshal?"

"Well, the gent I was talking about told me the whole story earlier today, after I arrested him for trying to pull another holdup."

Creighton stared at him, flabbergasted, and the spectators buzzed with talk until the judge gaveled them to silence. Janice and Estelle were both smiling now.

When Walton had things under control again, he said, "The prosecution's objection is overruled. Marshal, do you have the man you spoke of in custody?"

Longarm nodded. "Yes, Your Honor. He's out in the hall, under guard."

Walton signaled to the bailiff. "Bring in whoever's out there."

A moment later, Howard Summerlin, still in range clothes that looked out of place on him and with the colorful bandanna still draped around his neck, was brought into the courtroom. Natalie Malone gasped as she saw him. That was just the beginning of the uproar.

It took almost five minutes for Walton to quiet things down this time. Finally, he was able to say to Longarm, "Is it your testimony, Marshal, that this man plotted the robberies of his employer's silver shipments and then killed Mr. Malone when his malfeasance was discovered?"

"I reckon that's about the size of it, Your Honor," Longarm said with a nod.

Abercrombie Creighton was gaping like everyone else in the courtroom except for Longarm, Janice, and Estelle. Creighton's mouth opened and closed several times, making him look a little like a fish. Then he said, "But that's not possible! Malone's body was found in front of the desk. If Malone knew that Summerlin was stealing from him, he would have been on his guard. He would have kept the desk between them, and he wouldn't have allowed Summerlin to simply pick up that knife and stab him."

Longarm shrugged. "Summerlin didn't pick up the knife from the desk. Malone did. He came around the desk to go after Summerlin."

Summerlin had been staring at the floor, seemingly stunned, but now he showed some signs of life. He looked up and shouted, "It was self-defense! He tried to kill me! I . . . I had to fight back."

"Once you got the knife away from him, you didn't have to shove it in his chest," Longarm said. "But you saw a chance to get rid of a threat. You figured to blame the killing on Mrs. Malone, and then your stranglehold on Malone's holdings would be even stronger because Natalie would depend on you to run things."

Summerlin lifted his hands and buried his face in them, swaying back and forth a little as he groaned.

Creighton did his best to recover. "Your Honor," he said to Walton, "are we supposed to believe that this . . . this mouse of a man took a knife away from Jericho Malone, who was almost twice his size, and then killed him with it? Surely such a thing is so far-fetched, so beyond the reach of the imagination—"

"I got a lump on my jaw where Summerlin landed a punch earlier today," Longarm broke in. "When a fella's fightin' for his life, he's stronger than you think he'd be."

Walton said, "You apprehended Mr. Summerlin in the commission of one of these robberies, Marshal?"

"That's right. He never went along on one of the hold-ups until today, but he thought this would be an easy one, and the gang was short-handed because I'd ventilated a bunch of 'em over the past few days."

"I'll take your word for that," Walton said dryly. He turned to Janice. "Counselor, do you have a motion to make?"

Her chin came up. "Yes, Your Honor, I do. I move that the charge against my client, Mrs. Estelle Malone, be dismissed."

"Mr. Creighton?"

For a second, Creighton looked like he wanted to argue the matter. But then he sighed, clearly recognizing the inevitable, and said, "The prosecution makes no objection."

Walton lifted his gavel. "Motion granted. The charge

of murder against Mrs. Malone is dismissed." The gavel came down with a sharp crack.

The sound unleashed pandemonium in the room. Even though he hadn't been excused, Longarm figured it was all right for him to step down from the witness stand. He made his way through the crowd around the defense table, and Janice pushed forward to meet him. She threw her arms around his waist and cried, "You did it, Custis! You did it!"

"Not without a lot of help." He grinned down into her lovely face. "I don't reckon I ever saw a lawyer hug a witness before."

"Keep your eyes open," she said, returning his grin, "and you might just see a lot of things lawyers don't normally do with their star witnesses."

Chapter 22

The champagne glasses clinked together. "Here's to victory," Janice said.

"To justice," amended Longarm. He smiled at Estelle Malone, who sat with him and Janice at the table in one of Denver's finest restaurants.

"Thank you both," Estelle said when they had all sipped from their glasses. "Without you, I . . . I don't know what I'd have done."

"Summerlin would have slipped up sooner or later," Longarm said. "He was in over his head. But that lady-friend of his kept egging him on, and I reckon he figured he had to do whatever she said or risk losing her."

"The police haven't found her yet?" Janice asked.

Longarm shook his head. "Nope, but I reckon they will. Dan Hubbard don't like being wrong. He'll do everything he can now to set things right."

Janice laughed. "I'm afraid Mr. Creighton will never forgive you for stealing a conviction away from him, Marshal." Here in the restaurant, at this celebratory dinner, she was being a bit more formal than Longarm expected she would be later in the evening, when they were alone.

"Creighton'll get over it," said Longarm. "He's a windbag, but deep down he wants justice to be done, too. He'll just have to convict Summerlin and Belle Cardwell when they come to trial."

Estelle shook her head. "I can't believe that woman came to you and pretended to be Jericho's mistress, Marshal Long. What a terrible thing to do."

"She was just trying to sew up the case against you, Mrs. Malone. It didn't take, though."

Estelle looked down at the table and said ruefully, "I'm afraid I really did make poor Jericho's life miserable too much of the time. I . . . I've always had trouble with jealousy."

Janice patted the hand of her former client. "What's done is done, Estelle," she said quietly. "You can't change the past."

"No, but you can regret it. You can regret it for the rest of your life . . . but you're right. It doesn't change a thing." Estelle gave a slight shake of her head. "I'm sorry. Look at me, throwing cold water on what's supposed to be a celebration."

Longarm glanced past her and said, "Looks like you ain't the only one."

Janice and Estelle turned and saw Natalie Malone making her way across the crowded room toward their table. Natalie wore a stiff, determined expression on her face.

"Hello, Estelle," she said as she came up to the table. She barely glanced at Longarm and Janice and didn't acknowledge them otherwise. She went on, "I suppose you think you have the upper hand now."

"I don't want to fight with you, Natalie," Estelle said. "Life is too short for that. I realize that now."

"That's a pity, because we each own half of Father's estate, and I don't see us getting along too well. I've come to buy you out. I'll give you a fair price."

That seemed like the best solution to Longarm, but the decision was up to Estelle, of course. She hesitated, and he thought she was going to refuse Natalie's offer, but then she said, "This isn't the place to discuss it. Come see me at my hotel tomorrow, and we'll come to an arrangement."

Natalie nodded curtly. "Fine." She turned to walk away, adding coldly over her shoulder, "Good night."

Estelle sighed. "After everything that's happened, I don't think I want to stay in Denver anyway. But I'm worried that she's taking on too much. She's still a young woman."

"So's Janice," Longarm pointed out, "but she handled a big murder trial just fine."

"Thank you for the compliment, Marshal," Janice said. "I couldn't have done it without your help, though."

"I'm grateful to both of you," Estelle said. "You've given me back my freedom, my life. I can't thank you enough."

"Live it the best you can," Longarm told her. "That's thanks a-plenty."

They lay side by side in the big, soft bed, fondling each other's nude body. Longarm ran his big hands over Janice's slender form while she filled one hand with his erect organ and used the other to gently manipulate the heavy sac beneath it.

"I'll miss you so much, Custis," she whispered. Tears shone in her eyes.

"Shhh," Longarm said. "Don't think about that. All we really have is the here and now."

He put his arms around her hips and cupped her bottom, then rolled onto his back and took her with him so that she lay sprawled atop him. Their mouths found each other in a hungry kiss. Their tongues slithered and darted around each other playfully.

After a few moments, Janice sat up, straddling Longarm's thighs. His shaft jutted up in front of her belly. She stroked it a few times, then used her thumb to spread the drops of fluid that had seeped from the slit in its crown. The caress made Longarm's hips lift from the bed.

Smiling, Janice raised her hips and poised the opening

between her legs over Longarm's manhood. She guided it home as she settled down slowly, taking in more and more of the long, thick pole, until all of it was buried inside her. She let out a heartfelt sigh as she hit bottom, completely filled.

She sat like that for several moments, rocking back and forth slightly, obviously enjoying the sensation. Longarm reached up and stroked her breasts as she rode him. Janice's hips began to pump back and forth. Her movements were slow, deliberate, and sensuous. This time of passion was going to last as long as it possibly could.

She bent forward onto his chest, giving him more room to slide in and out of her. His arms went around her, holding her close. They kissed again.

Despite their good intentions, eventually their need for culmination grew too strong to be resisted. Longarm began thrusting faster and harder. Janice sat up again so that he could penetrate her to the deepest possible depths. She panted as her hips moved to match his thrusts.

"Now!" she gasped. "Fill me now, Custis!"

Longarm took hold of her hips and drove up into her, holding himself in place as he began to spasm. His thick seed erupted inside her, filling her as she demanded. Janice cried out as her own climax rippled through her.

She sagged forward again onto his chest as she relaxed in the aftermath of their lovemaking. Gently, Longarm stroked her hair, her back, and her hips as he kissed her mouth, nose, and forehead. It was a sweet, sweet moment for both of them . . .

Which just made it all the more jarring when the door of the hotel room burst open and a shrill voice screamed, "You ruined everything! I'll kill you!"

Longarm let his instincts take over. His arms tightened around Janice, and he rolled fast, taking her with him and falling off the side of the bed as a gun blasted twice. Janice cried out in fear and surprise.

They landed hard on the floor beside the bed, with Longarm on the bottom. That was a problem, because he couldn't reach his gun from here, and a wild-eyed Belle Cardwell was rushing around the bed, brandishing the revolver she had just used to try to kill him and Janice. Longarm grabbed the only weapon close at hand, which happened to be the unused porcelain chamber pot under the bed.

He flung the pot at Belle, and his aim was good. It struck her gun hand, shattering against the metal of the weapon. But the crash knocked the gun loose, too, and it slipped from Belle's fingers to thud to the floor.

Janice rolled over and came to her feet in a flash of creamy flesh. She threw as pretty a right cross as Longarm had ever seen from a woman, and her small fist cracked perfectly into Belle's jaw. Belle went flying backward. Her feet got tangled in the legs of a chair, and she fell, smashing the chair and landing on the floor in the middle of the wreckage. She groaned, her eyes rolling up in her head as she lost consciousness.

Janice stood there, naked but fierce, fists clenched, ready to strike again if it was necessary. It wasn't. All the fight had gone out of Belle.

Longarm got up and wrapped the comforter around Janice's nudity. Already there were hurrying footsteps and worried voices in the hall as people came to see what all the shooting had been about. As Longarm reached for his trousers and jammed his legs into them, he chuckled and asked, "Where'd you learn to throw a punch like that, Counselor?"

"My father taught me," Janice said. "In his younger days, he was a bit of a prizefighter, and I pestered him until he taught me how to box. Just like I made him teach me the law. I didn't have to argue very hard with him. He never thought being a woman should hold me back from anything I wanted to do."

"You are a barrel of surprises, Miss Parmalee. Next thing you'll be telling me is that you can use a gun, too."

"How do you know I can't?" asked Janice.

Longarm didn't answer that. He just returned the grin

that Janice gave him and reached down to haul the mostly senseless Belle Cardwell to her feet. The police would be here any minute, and he would turn Belle over to them.

Then the rest of the night would belong to him and Janice. He figured they both had some more motions they still wanted to make.